Deemed 'the father of the scientifi
Austin Freeman had a long and distinguished career, not least as
a writer of detective fiction. He was born in London, the son of a
tailor who went on to train as a pharmacist. After graduating as a
surgeon at the Middlesex Hospital Medical College, Freeman
taught for a while and joined the colonial service, offering his skills
as an assistant surgeon along the Gold Coast of Africa. He became
embroiled in a diplomatic mission when a British expeditionary
party was sent to investigate the activities of the French. Through
his tact and formidable intelligence, a massacre was narrowly
avoided. His future was assured in the colonial service. However,
after becoming ill with blackwater fever, Freeman was sent back to
England to recover and, finding his finances precarious, embarked
on a career as acting physician in Holloway Prison. In desperation,
he turned to writing and went on to dominate the world of
British detective fiction, taking pride in testing different criminal
techniques. So keen were his powers as a writer that part of one of
his best novels was written in a bomb shelter.

BY THE SAME AUTHOR
ALL PUBLISHED BY HOUSE OF STRATUS

THE FURTHER ADVENTURES
OF ROMNEY PRINGLE

R Austin Freeman

HOUSE OF
STRATUS

This edition published in 2001 by House of Stratus, an imprint of Stratus Holdings plc, 24c Old Burlington Street, London, W1X 1RL, UK. Also at: Suite 210, 1270 Avenue of the Americas, New York, NY 10020, USA.

www.houseofstratus.com

Typeset, printed and bound by House of Stratus.

A catalogue record for this book is available from the British Library and the Library of Congress.

ISBN 0-7551-0346-7

CONTENTS

The Submarine Boat

Tric-trac! tric-trac! went the black and white discs as the players moved them over the backgammon board in expressive justification of the French term for the game. Tric-trac! They are indeed a nation of poets, reflected Mr Pringle. Was not Teuf-teuf! for the motor car a veritable inspiration? And as he smoked, the not unmusical clatter of the enormous wooden discs filled the atmosphere.

In these days of cookery not entirely based upon air-tights – to use the expressive Americanism for tinned meats – it is no longer necessary for the man who wishes to dine, as distinguished from the mere feeding animal, to furtively seek some restaurant in remote Soho, jealously guarding its secret from his fellows. But Mr Pringle, in his favourite study of human nature, was an occasional visitor to the "Poissonnerie" in Gerrard Street, and, the better to pursue his researches, had always denied familiarity with the foreign tongues he heard around him. The restaurant was distinctly close – indeed, some might have called it stuffy – and Pringle, though near a ventilator, thoughtfully provided by the management, was fast being lulled into drowsiness, when a man who had taken his seat with a companion at the next table leaned across the intervening gulf and addressed him.

"Nous ne vous dérangeons pas, monsieur?" Pringle, with a smile of fatuous uncomprehending, bowed, but said never a word.

"Cochon d'Anglais, n'entendez-vous pas?"

1

"I'm afraid I do not understand," returned Pringle, shaking his head hopelessly, but still smiling.

"Canaille! Faut-il que je vous tire le nez?" persisted the Frenchman, as, apparently still sceptical of Pringle's assurance, he added threats to abuse.

"I have known the English gentleman a long time, and without a doubt he does not understand French," testified the waiter who had now come forward for orders. Satisfied by this corroboration of Pringle's innocence, the Frenchman bowed and smiled sweetly to him, and, ordering a bottle of *Clos de Vougeot*, commenced an earnest conversation with his neighbour.

By the time this little incident had closed, Pringle's drowsiness had given place to an intense feeling of curiosity. For what purpose could the Frenchman have been so insistent in disbelieving his expressed ignorance of the language? Why, too, had he striven to make Pringle betray himself by resenting the insults showered upon him? In a Parisian restaurant, as he knew, far more trivial affronts had ended in meetings in the Bois de Boulogne. Besides, *cochon* was an actionable term of opprobrium in France.

The Frenchman and his companion had seated themselves at the only vacant table, also it was in a corner; Pringle, at the next, was the single person within earshot, and the Frenchman's extraordinary behaviour could only be due to a consuming thirst for privacy. Settling himself in an easy position, Pringle closed his eyes, and while appearing to resume his slumber, strained every nerve to discern the slightest word that passed at the next table. Dressed in the choicest mode of Piccadilly, the Frenchman bore himself with all the intolerable self-consciousness of the Boulevardier; but there was no trace of good-natured levity in the dark aquiline features, and the evil glint of the eyes recalled visions of an operatic Mephistopheles. His guest was unmistakably an Englishman of the bank-clerk type, who contributed his share of the conversation in halting Anglo-French, punctuated by nervous laughter as, with agonizing pains, he dredged his memory for elusive colloquialisms.

Freely translated, this was what Pringle heard:

"So your people have really decided to take up the submarine, after all?"

"Yes; I am working out the details of some drawings in small-scale."

"But are they from headquarters?"

"Certainly! Duly initialled and passed by the chief constructor."

"And you are making – "

"Full working drawings."

"There will be no code or other secret about them?"

"What I am doing can be understood by any naval architect."

"Ah, an English one?"

"The measurements, of course, are English, but they are easily convertible."

"You could do that?"

"Too dangerous! Suppose a copy in metric scale were found in my possession! Besides, any draughtsman could reduce them in an hour or two."

"And when can you let me have it?"

"In about two weeks."

"Impossible! I shall not be here."

"Unless something happens to let me get on with it quickly, I don't see how I can do it even then. I am never sufficiently free from interruption to take tracings; there are far too many eyes upon me. The only chance I have is to spoil the thing as soon as I have the salient points worked out on it, and after I have pretended to destroy it, smuggle it home; then I shall have to work out the details from them in the evening. It is simply impossible for me to attempt to take a finished drawing out of the yard, and, as it is, I don't quite see my way to getting the spoilt one out – they look so sharply after spoilt drawings."

"Two weeks you say, then?"

"Yes; and I shall have to sit up most nights copying the day's work from my notes to do it."

"Listen! In a week I must attend at the Ministry of Marine in Paris, but our military attaché is my friend. I can trust him; he shall come down to you."

"What, at Chatham? Do you wish to ruin me?" A smile from the Frenchman. "No; it must be in London, where no one knows me."

"Admirable! My friend will be better able to meet you."

"Very well, as soon as I am ready I will telegraph to you."

"Might not the address of the embassy be remarked by the telegraph officials? Your English post office is charmingly unsuspicious, but we must not risk anything."

"Ah, perhaps so. Well, I will come up to London and telegraph to you from here. But your representative – will he be prepared for it?"

"I will warn him to expect it in fourteen days." He made an entry in his pocketbook. "How will you sign the message?"

"Gustave Zede," suggested the Englishman, sniggering for the first and only time.

"Too suggestive. Sign yourself 'Pauline', and simply add the time."

" 'Pauline', then. Where shall the rendezvous be?"

"The most public place we can find."

"Public?"

"Certainly. Some place where everyone will be too much occupied with his own affairs to notice you. What say you to your Nelson's Column? There you can wait in a way we shall agree upon."

"It would be a difficult thing for me to wear a disguise."

"All disguises are clumsy unless one is an expert. Listen! You shall be gazing at the statue with one hand in your breast – so."

"Yes; and I might hold a 'Baedeker' in my other hand."

"Admirable, my friend! You have the true spirit of an artist," sneered the Frenchman.

"Your representative will advance and say to me, 'Pauline', and the exchange can be made without another word."

"Exchange?"

"I presume your Government is prepared to pay me handsomely for the very heavy risks I am running in this matter," said the Englishman stiffly.

"Pardon, my friend! How imbecile of me! I am authorized to offer you ten thousand francs."

A pause, during which the Englishman made a calculation on the back of an envelope.

"That is four hundred pounds," he remarked, tearing the envelope into carefully minute fragments. "Far too little for such a risk."

"Permit me to remind you, my friend, that you came in search of me, or rather of those I represent. You have something to sell? Good! But it is customary for the merchant to display his wares first."

"I pledge myself to give you copies of the working drawings made for the use of artificers themselves. I have already met you oftener than is prudent. As I say, you offer too little."

"Should the drawings prove useless to us, we should, of course, return them to your Admiralty, explaining how they came into our possession." There was an unpleasant smile beneath the Frenchman's waxed moustache as he spoke. "What sum do you ask?"

"Five hundred pounds in small notes – say, five pounds each."

"That is – what do you say? Ah, twelve thousand five hundred francs! Impossible! My limit is twelve thousand."

To this the Englishman at length gave an ungracious consent, and after some adroit compliments, beneath which the other sought to bury his implied threat, the pair rose from the table. Either by accident or design, the Frenchman stumbled over the feet of Pringle, who, with his long legs stretching out from under the table, his head bowed and his lips parted, appeared in a profound slumber. Opening his eyes slowly, he feigned a lifelike yawn, stretched his arms, and gazed lazily around, to the entire satisfaction of the Frenchman, who, in the act of parting with his companion, was watching him from the door.

Calling for some coffee, Pringle lighted a cigarette, and reflected with a glow of indignant patriotism upon the sordid transaction he had become privy to. It is seldom that public servants are in this country found ready to betray their trust – with all honour be it recorded of them! But there ever exists the possibility of some underpaid official succumbing to the temptation at the command of the less scrupulous representatives of foreign powers, whose actions in this respect are always ignored officially by their superiors. To Pringle's somewhat cynical imagination, the sordid huckstering of a dockyard draughtsman with a French naval attaché appealed as corroboration of Walpole's famous principle, and as he walked homeward to Furnival's Inn, the seat of his fictitious literary agency, he determined, if possible, to turn his discovery to the mutual advantage of his country and himself – especially the latter.

During the next few days Pringle elaborated a plan of taking up a residence at Chatham, only to reject it as he had done many previous ones. Indeed, so many difficulties presented themselves to every single course of action, that the tenth day after found him strolling down Bond Street in the morning without having taken any further step in the matter. With his characteristic fastidious neatness in personal matters, he was bound for the Piccadilly establishment of the chief and, for West-Enders, the only firm of hatters in London.

"Breton Stret, do you knoh?" said a voice suddenly. And Pringle, turning, found himself accosted by a swarthy foreigner.

"Bruton Street, n'est-ce pas?" Pringle suggested.

"Mais oui, Brruten Stret, monsieur!" was the reply in faint echo of the English syllables.

"Le voilà! à droite," was Pringle's glib direction. Politely raising his hat in response to the other's salute, he was about to resume his walk when he noticed that the Frenchman had been joined by a companion, who appeared to have been making similar inquiries.

The latter started and uttered a slight exclamation on meeting Pringle's eye. The recognition was mutual — it was the French attaché! As he hurried down Bond Street, Pringle realized with acutest annoyance that his deception at the restaurant had been unavailing, while he must now abandon all hope of a counterplot for the honour of his country, to say nothing of his own profit. The port-wine mark on his right cheek was far too conspicuous for the attaché not to recognize him by it, and he regretted his neglect to remove it as soon as he had decided to follow up the affair. Forgetful of all beside, he walked on into Piccadilly, and it was not until he found himself more than half-way back to his chambers that he remembered the purpose for which he had set out; but matters of greater moment now claimed his attention, and he endeavoured by the brisk exercise to work off some of the chagrin with which he was consumed. Only as he reached the Inn and turned into the gateway did it occur to him that he had been culpably careless in thus going straight homeward. What if he had been followed? Never in his life had he shown such disregard for ordinary precautions. Glancing back, he just caught a glimpse of a figure which seemed to whip behind the corner of the gateway. He retraced his steps and looked out into Holborn.

There, in the very act of retreat, and still but a few feet from the gate, was the attaché himself. Cursing the persistence of his own folly, Pringle dived through the arch again, and, determined that the Frenchman should discover no more that day, he turned nimbly to the left and ran up his own stairway before the pursuer could have time to re-enter the Inn.

The most galling reflection was his absolute impotence in the matter. Through lack of the most elementary foresight he had been fairly run to earth, and could see no way of ridding himself of this unwelcome attention. To transfer his domicile, to tear himself up by the roots as it were, was out of the question; and as he glanced around him, from the soft carpets and luxurious chairs to the warm, distempered walls with their old prints above the dado of dwarf bookcases, he felt that the pang of severance from the refined associations of his chambers would be too acute. Besides, he would inevitably be tracked elsewhere. He would gain nothing by the transfer. One thing at least was absolutely certain – the trouble which the Frenchman was taking to watch him showed the importance he attached to Pringle's discovery. But this again only increased his disgust with the ill luck which had met him at the very outset. After all, he had done nothing illegal, however contrary it might be to the code of ethics, so that if it pleased them the entire French legation might continue to watch him till the Day of Judgement, and, consoling himself with this reflection, he philosophically dismissed the matter from his mind.

It was nearing six when he again left the Inn for Pagani's, the Great Portland Street restaurant which he much affected; instead of proceeding due west, he crossed Holborn, intending to bear round by way of the Strand and Regent Street, and so get up an appetite.

In Staple Inn he paused a moment in the further archway. The little square, always reposeful amid the stress and turmoil of its environment, seemed doubly so this evening, its eighteenth-century calm so welcome after the raucous thoroughfare. An approaching footfall echoed noisily, and as Pringle moved from the shadow of the narrow wall the newcomer hesitated and stopped, and then made the circuit of the square, scanning the doorways as if in search of a name. The action was not unnatural, and twenty-four hours earlier Pringle would have thought nothing of it, but after the events of the morning he endowed it with a personal interest, and, walking on, he ascended the steps into Southampton Buildings and stopped by a hoarding.

As he looked back he was rewarded by the sight of a man stealthily emerging from the archway and making his way up the steps, only to halt as he suddenly came abreast of Pringle. Although his face was unfamiliar, Pringle could only conclude that the man was following him, and all doubt was removed when, having walked along the street and turning about at the entrance to

Chancery Lane, he saw the spy had resumed the chase and was now but a few yards back.

Pringle, as a philosopher, felt more inclined to laughter than resentment at this ludicrous espionage. In a spirit of mischief, he pursued his way to the Strand at a tortoise-like crawl, halting as if doubtful of his way at every corner, and staring into every shop whose lights still invited customers. Once or twice he even doubled back, and passing quite close to the man had several opportunities of examining him. He was quite unobtrusive, even respectable-looking; there was nothing of the foreigner about him, and Pringle shrewdly conjectured that the attaché, wearied of sentry-go, had turned it over to some English servant on whom he could rely.

Thus shepherded, Pringle arrived at the restaurant, from which he only emerged after a stay maliciously prolonged over each item of the menu, followed by the smoking of no fewer than three cigars of a brand specially lauded by the proprietor.

With a measure of humanity diluting his malice, he was about to offer the infallibly exhausted sentinel some refreshment when he came out, but as the man was invisible, Pringle started for home, taking much the same route as before, and calmly debating whether or no the cigars he had just sampled would be a wise investment; not until he had reached Southampton Buildings and the sight of the hoarding recalled the spy's discomfiture, did he think of looking back to see if he were still followed. All but the main thoroughfares were by this time deserted, and although he shot a keen glance up and down Chancery Lane, now clear of all but the most casual traffic, not a soul was anywhere near him.

By a curious psychological process Pringle felt inclined to resent the man's absence. He had begun to regard him almost in the light of a bodyguard, the private escort of some eminent politician. Besides, the whole incident was pregnant with possibilities appealing to his keenly intellectual sense of humour, and as he passed the hoarding, he peered into its shadow with the half-admitted hope that his attendant might be lurking in the depths.

Later on he recalled how, as he glanced upwards, a man's figure passed like a shadow from a ladder to an upper platform of the scaffold. The vision, fleeting and unsubstantial, had gone almost before his retina had received it, but the momentary halt was to prove his salvation.

Even as he turned to walk on, a cataract of planks, amid scaffold poles and a chaos of loose bricks, crashed on the spot he was about to traverse; a stray beam, more erratic in its descent, caught his hat, and, telescoping it, glanced off his shoulder, bearing him to the ground, where he lay dazed by the sudden uproar and half-choked by the cloud of dust.

Rapid and disconcerting as was the event, he remembered afterwards a slim and spectral shape approaching through the gloom. In a dreamy kind of way he connected it with that other shadow figure he had seen high up on the scaffold, and as it bent over him he recognized the now familiar features of the spy. But other figures replaced the first, and, when helped to his feet, he made futile search for it amid the circle of faces gathered round him. He judged it an hallucination. By the time he had undergone a tentative dust-down he was sufficiently collected to acknowledge the sympathetic congratulations of the crowd and to decline the homeward escort of a constable.

In the privacy of his chambers, his ideas began to clarify. Events arranged themselves in logical sequence, and the spectres assumed more tangible form.

A single question dwarfed all others. He asked himself, "Was the cataclysm such an accident as it appeared?" And as he surveyed the battered ruins of his hat, he began to realize how nearly had he been the victim of a murderous vendetta!

When he arose the next morning, he scarcely needed the dilapidated hat to remind him of the events of yesterday. Normally a sound and dreamless sleeper, his rest had been a series of short snatches of slumber interposed between longer spells of rumination. While he marvelled at the intensity of malice which he could no longer doubt pursued him – a vindictiveness more natural to a mediaeval Italian state than to this present-day metropolis – he bitterly regretted the fatal curiosity which had brought him to such an extremity.

By no means deficient in the grosser forms of physical courage, his sense that in the game which was being played, his adversaries, as unscrupulous as they were crafty, held all the cards, and, above all, that their espionage effectually prevented him filling the gaps in the plot which he had as yet only half-discovered, was especially galling to his active and somewhat neurotic temperament.

Until yesterday he had almost decided to drop the affair of the Restaurant "Poissonnerie", but now, after what he firmly believed to be a deliberate attempt to assassinate him, he realized the desperate situation of a duellist with his back to a wall – having scarce room to parry, he felt the prick of his antagonist's rapier deliberately goading him to an incautious thrust. Was he regarded as the possessor of a dangerous secret? Then it behoved him to strike, and that without delay.

Now that he was about to attack, a disguise was essential; and reflecting how lamentably he had failed through the absence of one hitherto, he removed the port-wine mark from his right cheek with his customary spirit lotion, and blackened his fair hair with a few smart applications of a preparation from his bureau. It was with a determination to shun any obscure streets or alleys, and especially all buildings in course of erection, that he started out after his usual light breakfast.

At first he was doubtful whether he was being followed or not, but after a few experimental turns and doublings he was unable to single out any regular attendant of his walk; either his disguise had proved effectual or his enemies imagined that the attempt of last night had been less innocent in its results.

Somewhat soothed by this discovery, Pringle had gravitated towards the Strand and was nearing Charing Cross, when he observed a man cross from the station to the opposite corner carrying a brown-paper roll. With his thoughts running in the one direction, Pringle in a flash recognized the dockyard draughtsman. Could he be even now on his way to keep the appointment at Nelson's Column? Had he been warned of Pringle's discovery, and so expedited his treacherous task? And thus reflecting, Pringle determined at all hazards to follow him.

The draughtsman made straight for the telegraph office. It was now the busiest time of the morning, most of the little desks were occupied by more or less glib message-writers, and the draughtsman had found a single vacancy at the far end when Pringle followed him in and reached over his shoulder to withdraw a form from the rack in front of him.

Grabbing three or four, Pringle neatly spilled them upon the desk, and with an abject apology hastily gathered them up together with the form the draughtsman was employed upon. More apologies, and Pringle, seizing a suddenly vacant desk, effected to compose a telegram of his own. The draughtsman's message had been short, and (to Pringle) exceptionally sweet, consisting as it did of three words – "Four-thirty, Pauline." The address Pringle had not attempted to read – he knew that already.

The moment the other left Pringle took up a sheaf of forms, and, as if they had been the sole reason for his visit, hurried out of the office and took a hansom back to Furnival's Inn.

Here his first care was to fold some newspapers into a brown-paper parcel resembling the one carried by the draughtsman as nearly as he remembered it, and having cut a number of squares of stiff tissue paper, he stuffed an envelope with them and pondered over a cigarette the most difficult stage of his campaign. Twice had the draughtsman seen him.

Once at the restaurant, in his official guise as the sham literary agent, with smooth face, fair hair, and the fugitive port-wine mark staining his right cheek; again that morning, with blackened hair and unblemished face. True, he might have forgotten the stranger at the restaurant; on the other hand, he might not – and Pringle was then (as always) steadfastly averse to leaving anything to chance. Besides, in view of this sudden journey to London, it was very likely that he had received warning of Pringle's discovery. Lastly, it was more than probable that the spy was still on duty, even though he had failed to recognize Pringle that morning.

The matter was clinched by a single glance at the Venetian mirror above the mantel, which reflected a feature he had overlooked – his now blackened hair. Nothing remained for him but to assume a disguise which should impose on both the spy and the draughtsman, and after some thought he decided to make up as a Frenchman of the South, and to pose as a servant of the French embassy.

Reminiscent of the immortal Tartarin, his ready bureau furnished him with a stiff black moustache and some specially stout horsehair to typify the stubbly beard of that hero. When, at almost a quarter to four, he descended into the Inn with the parcel in his hand, a Baedeker and the envelope of tissues in his pocket, a cab was just setting down, and impulsively he chartered it as far as Exeter Hall. Concealed in the cab, he imagined he would the more readily escape observation, and, by the time he alighted, flattered himself that any pursuit had been baffled.

As he discharged the cab, however, he noticed a hansom draw up a few paces in the rear, whilst a man got out and began to saunter westward behind him. His suspicions alert, although the man was certainly a stranger, Pringle at once put him to the test by entering Romano's and ordering a small whisky.

After a decent delay, he emerged, and his pulse quickened when he saw a couple of doors off the same man staring into a shop window! Pringle walked a few yards back, and then crossed to the opposite side of the street, but although he dodged at infinite peril through a string of omnibuses, he was unable to shake off his satellite, who, with unswerving persistence, occupied the most limited horizon whenever he looked back.

For almost the first time in his life, Pringle began to despair. The complacent regard of his own precautions had proved but a fool's paradise. Despite his elaborate disguise, he must have been plainly recognizable to his enemies, and he began to ask himself whether it was not useless to struggle further.

As he paced slowly on, an indefinable depression stole over him. He thought of the heavy price so nearly exacted for his interposition. Resentment surged over him at the memory, and his hand clenched on the parcel. The contact furnished the very stimulus he required. The instrument of settling such a score was in his hands, and rejecting his timorous doubts, he strode on, determined to make one bold and final stroke for vengeance.

The shadows had lengthened appreciably, and the quarter chiming from near St Martin's warned him that there was no time to lose – the spy must be got rid of at any cost. Already could he see the estuary of the Strand, with the Square widening beyond; on his right loomed the tunnel of the Lowther Arcade, with its vista of juvenile delights.

The sight was an inspiration. Darting in, he turned off sharp to the left into an artist's repository, with a double entrance to the Strand and the Arcade, and, softly closing the door, peeped through the palettes and frames which hung upon the glass. Hardly had they ceased swinging to his movement when he had the satisfaction of seeing the spy, the scent already cold, rush furiously up the Arcade, his course marked by falling toys and the cries of the outraged stall keepers.

Turning, Pringle made the purchase of a sketching-block, the first thing handy, and then passed through the door which gave on the Strand. At the post office he stopped to survey the scene. A single policeman stood by the eastward base of the column, and the people scattered round seemed but ordinary wayfarers, but just across the maze of traffic was a spectacle of intense interest to him.

At the quadrant of the Grand Hotel, patrolling aimlessly in front of the shops, at which he seemed too perturbed to stare for more than a few seconds at a time, the draughtsman kept palpitating vigil until the clock should strike the half-hour of his treason. True to the Frenchman's advice, he sought safety in a crowd, avoiding the desert of the square until the last moment.

It wanted two minutes to the half-hour when Pringle opened his Baedeker, and, thrusting one hand into his breast, examined the statue and coil of rope erected to the glory of our greatest hero. "Pauline!" said a voice, with the musical inflection unattainable by any but a Frenchman. Beside him stood a slight, neatly dressed young man, with close-cropped hair, and a moustache and imperial, who cast a significant look at the parcel.

Pringle immediately held it towards him and, the dark gentleman producing an envelope from his breast pocket, the exchange was effected in silence. With bows and a raising of hats they parted, while Big Ben boomed on his eight bells.

The attaché's representative had disappeared some minutes beyond the westernmost lion before the draughtsman appeared from the opposite direction, his uncertain steps intermitted by frequent halts and nervous backward glances. With his back to the National Gallery he produced a Baedeker and commenced to stare up at the monument, withdrawing his eyes every now and then to cast a shamefaced look to right and left.

In his agitation the draughtsman had omitted the hand-in-the-breast attitude, and even as Pringle advanced to his side and murmured "Pauline", his legs (almost stronger than his will) seemed to be urging him to a flight from the field of dishonour.

With tremulous eagerness he thrust a brown-paper parcel into Pringle's hands, and, snatching the envelope of tissue slips, rushed across the road and disappeared in the bar of the Grand Hotel.

Pringle turned to go, but was confronted by a revolver, and as his eye traversed the barrel and met that of its owner, he recognized the Frenchman to whom he had just sold the bundle of newspapers. Dodging the weapon, he tried to spring into the open, but a restraining grip on each elbow held him in the angle of the plinth, and turning ever so little Pringle found himself in custody of the man whom he had last seen in full cry up the Lowther Arcade.

No constable was anywhere near, and even casual passengers walked unheeding by the nook, so quiet was the progress of this little drama. Lowering his revolver, the dark gentleman picked up the parcel which had fallen from Pringle in the struggle. He opened it with delicacy, partially withdrew some sheets of tracing paper, which he intently examined, and then placed the whole in an inner pocket, and, giving a sign to the spy to loose his grasp, he spoke for the first time.

"May I suggest, sir," he said in excellent English with the slightest foreign accent, "may I suggest that in the future you do not meddle with what cannot possibly concern you? These documents have been bought and sold, and although you have been good enough to act as intermediary in the transaction, I can assure you we were under no necessity of calling on you for your help."

Here his tone hardened, and, speaking with less calmness, the accent became more noticeable; "I discovered your impertinence in selling me a parcel of worthless papers very shortly after I left you. Had you succeeded in the attempt you appear to have planned so carefully, it is possible you might have lived long enough to regret it – perhaps not! I wish you good day, sir." He bowed, as did his companion, and Pringle, walking on, turned up by the corner of the Union Club.

Dent's clock marked twenty minutes to five, and Pringle reflected how much had been compressed into the last quarter of an hour. True, he had not prevented the sale of his country's secrets; on the other hand – he pressed the packet which held the envelope of notes. Hailing a cab, he was about to step in, when, looking back, at the nook between the lions he saw a confused movement about the spot.

The two men he had just left were struggling with a third, who, brandishing a handful of something white, was endeavouring, with varying success, to plant his fist on divers areas of their persons. He was the draughtsman.

A small crowd, which momentarily increased, surrounded them, and as Pringle climbed into the hansom two policemen were seen to penetrate the ring and impartially lay hands upon the three combatants.

The Kimberly Fugitive

"Westerly and south-westerly breezes, close, thunder locally."

Twenty times that day had Mr Pringle consulted the forecast, and then had tapped the barometer without inducing the pointer to travel beyond "change".

Indeed, as evening drew near with no sign of the promised storm, the prospect was quite sufficient to abate the philosophic calm which was his usual mask to the outer world. A morning drizzle had been so greedily licked by the scorching pavement, or lost in the sand and grit, that, inches deep, covered the roadway, that the plane trees on the Embankment, with a mottling where the rain had splashed their dusty leaves, were the sole evidence of a shower too fleeting to be remembered.

The drought was of many weeks' standing. The country lay roasting beneath a brazen sky, great fissures starred the earth, while a mat of peculiarly penetrating dust impartially floured the roads and hedges. London, with all its drawbacks, was more tolerable; at the least there was some shade to be found there, and Pringle had not yet been tempted from his chambers in Furnival's Inn.

When sunset came, and the daily traffic slackened, Pringle shouldered his cycle and carried it down the stone stairs from the second floor. His profession of the phantom literary agency, so gravely announced upon his door, allowed him to dress with a disregard of convention, and it was in a bluish flannel suit and straw hat that he pedalled along Holborn in the comparative coolness. By the bumpy slope of St Andrew's Hill and the equally rough pavement of New Bridge Street, he reached Blackfriars, and turned to the right along the Embankment; it ran in his mind to go as far West as possible, inhaling whatever ozone the breeze might carry, returning later with the wind behind him.

The seats, crowded with limp humanity, the silent children too tired even to play, the general listlessness and absence of stir, all witnessed to the consuming heat. The roadway was almost deserted, but just by the Temple Pringle was conscious of the disagreeable sensation so full of meaning to a cyclist, of something striking his back wheel. From behind there came an exclamation, an oath from between close ground teeth, and as he sprinted on and dismounted these were punctuated by a loud crash.

Pringle knew the meaning of it all without turning. The shock had been too gentle and withal noiseless to be caused by anything but another cycle, ridden most likely by some ground-gazing scorcher, and knowing that with even the best of riders a collision with another machine in front means disaster, he was quite prepared for what he saw.

A few yards back a dilapidated-looking cyclist was examining his mount. His dark hair and moustache had acquired the same grey tint as his clothing, so generously had he been coated with dust in what must have been a long ride; but the machine appeared to have suffered more from the fall than its rider, who dolefully handled a pedal which declined to revolve.

"Can I be of any help?" inquired Pringle with his usual suavity. "I hope there's nothing serious the matter."

"Pedal pin's bent, and I've hurt my ankle," returned the cyclist. He spoke shortly, as if inclined to blame Pringle for the accident due to his own folly.

"Is it a sprain?" asked Pringle sympathetically. "Do you think you can ride with it?"

"Nothing much, I think." He walked round the machine with a slight limp, and added surlily, "But I can't ride a thing like that." He indicated the pedal with a pettish finger as he raised the machine from the ground.

19

"Oh, I think a few minutes' work will put that right," observed Pringle encouragingly.

"No! Really?" He brightened visibly as if Pringle had rid him of a certain incubus.

"I don't think we shall find a repairer open now – besides I don't know of one just about here. If you will allow me, I'll see what I can do to put it right. As you say, you can't ride like that."

The stranger was obviously not a practical cyclist, and Pringle, leaning his own machine against the curb, had produced a spanner and was on his hands and knees beside the damaged cycle before the other had well got his pouch unstrapped. Pringle had put down his concern for the machine to the natural affection of an owner, but, with some of the dust and mud brushed off, it stood revealed as a hired crock, with cheap Belgian fittings. The dull enamel, the roughly machined lugs, the general lack of finish showed the second-rate machine; and it was no drop-forging which yielded to the persuasion of a very moderately powerful wrench, the soft steel straightening under the leverage almost as readily as it had bent.

Meanwhile, the owner vented an unamiable mood in dispersing the inevitable boys crowding like vultures round the fallen cycle; and when Pringle, his labour ended, struck his shoulder beneath the handlebar and was peppered with a shower of dust and pellets from the mudguards, he had lost some of his former incivility, and, producing a handkerchief, insisted on dusting his benefactor with quite a gracious air.

"I see you've ridden far," remarked Pringle as he finished.

"Yes; from – er – er – Colchester," was the hesitating reply.

"Suppose we move on a bit from this crowd?" Pringle suggested. "I think we are both going westwards."

"I was on the look out for a quiet hotel somewhere near here," said the cyclist as they rode side by side.

"I think the 'Embankment' in Arundel Street would suit you; it's moderate and quiet – round here to the right. By the bye, it's some time since I was on the Colchester Road, but I remember

what an awful hill there is at Hatfield Peverel. I don't know which
is the worst – to come up or go down."

"Hatfield – Hatfield Peverel?" repeated the other musingly.

"Just this side of Witham, you know. Why, surely you must have
noticed that hill!"

"Oh, yes. Witham – yes, a very nasty hill!"

"No, not Witham. You come to the hill at Hatfield Peverel."

"Yes, yes – I know." And then, as if anxious to change the
subject, "Are we anywhere near the hotel?"

"Just the other side of that red-brick building. I see you've
managed to pick up a little real estate on your way." The stranger
started and glanced suspiciously at Pringle, who explained, "The
mud, I mean."

"Oh! the mud. Ha! Ha! Ha!" There was more of hysteria than
hilarity in the laugh and the man suddenly grew voluble. "Yes, I
came through a lot of mud. Fact is, I was caught in the
thunderstorm."

"Indeed! That's good news. Whereabouts was it?"

"Near Tonbridge."

"Tonbridge?"

"Tut! What am I talking about? I mean Colchester. But this is
the place, isn't it? Goodnight – goodnight!" He dragged the
machine into the hotel, leaving Pringle to silently debate whether
his boorishness was due to his confusion, or his confusion to his
boorishness.

With his foot on the step, Pringle was just remounting when a
muffled rumble sounded overhead. The stars were hidden by a
huge inksplash, and a pallid, ghostly light flickered in the south;
then, with measured pat, huge blobs of rain began to fall, while a
blast, as from all the furnaces across the stream, blew up from the
Embankment. It was the long-deferred storm, and Pringle told
himself his ride must be abandoned; he had wasted too much time
over this ingrate.

Resigned to another night of stuffy insomnia, he turned and
pedalled up towards the Strand. Beside him ran a newsboy,
shouting his alliterative bill: "Storm in the south! Rain in rivers."

Cramming a pink sheet into his pocket Pringle hurried on, and reached Furnival's Inn as a blinding glare lit up the gateway, and the clouds exploded with a crackling volley.

Fagged and dusty, his head throbbing to the reverberation of the thunder, Pringle collapsed on his sofa and languidly unfolded the paper; but, at the first glance he sat up again with a start, for in the place of honour beneath the alliterative headlines he read: –

The Central News reports that a violent thunderstorm, which did some damage to the hop-fields, burst over the Tonbridge district early this afternoon. For a time many of the roads were impassable, the drains and ditches being choked by the sudden rush of stormwater. So far as is known no loss of life occurred. Further storms may be expected in the Home Counties and will be anxiously awaited by agriculturists.

"Tonbridge!" thought Pringle. "Was there no storm in Essex?" He scanned the rest of the paper with an eagerness which dismissed his fatigue. The cyclist had positively named Colchester as the scene of the storm. Strange that the paper said nothing about it – and there was ample time for the news to have reached London, too.

He flicked a crumb of dry mud out of his turned-up trousers, and recalled what an avalanche had poured from the stranger's machine. That was no passing shower it had sped through. Stay – why, of course! The man actually did say Tonbridge, and then made haste to correct himself. And how clumsily he made his escape afterwards! Supposing he had travelled up through Tonbridge he would probably cross Blackfriars Bridge, and thus his presence on the Embankment would be explained. But why had he told a lie about it? What could he possibly have to conceal?

Pringle absently turned the rest of the mud out of his trousers and threw up the window. With widespread fingers he cast the handful abroad, when a sudden inspiration bid him pause, and tightly clasping the remnants of dust, he took a sheet of paper and carefully scraped his palm over it. The "Britannica" stood ever ready to his hand, and taking a volume from its shelf he studied it intently for a while, murmuring, as he replaced it, "Essex, Thanet sands and London clay."

Across the room stood his oak bureau – the bureau which indifferently supplied an actor's make-up or a chemist's laboratory, and opening it, he drew out a test tube and a bottle of hydrochloric acid. Shaking the dust into the tube he poured the acid in and watched the turbid solution as it slowly clarified after a brisk effervescence; then with a steady hand he added a few drops of sulphuric acid and his impassive features relaxed in a grim smile as the resulting opalescence deepened to opacity, and this in turn condensed into a woolly cloud.

The delicate test established the presence of chalk and the entire absence of clay. Thus, for all his clumsy lying, science, which cannot be deceived, declared that the cyclist had ridden into London over chalky roads – that is to say, not from Essex, but from the south.

The storm had passed. Clear moonlight succeeded the lambent spasms of the lightning, and a cool breeze sang past the upper windows of the Inn. Physical weariness would not be denied, and with the novel prospect of an unbroken night's rest before him, Pringle abandoned any present attempt to learn the motive of the stranger's deception.

The sun was shining brightly between the green blind-slats when he awoke. Tired out, he had slept long past his usual hour. Lighting the spirit lamp to prepare his simple breakfast he glanced over the paper he found beneath his outer door. As he was accustomed to explain, he read the *Chronicle* not from any sympathy without its opinions, but as being the most really informing journal published in London.

The water boiled and boiled in the little kettle, the flame sputtered and died as the spirit burned out; but Pringle, intent on the newspaper, took no heed of his meal. There was barely a third of a column; but as he read and reread the paragraphs the

personality of the cyclist was ever before him, and remembering
the chemical analysis, his suspicions all crowded back again –
suspicions which he had laid aside with the headache of last night.

A TALE OF THE DIAMOND FIELDS

About a month ago, according to the South African papers
just to hand, some sensation was caused in Kimberly by the
disappearance of an outside broker named Thomas, who for
some time past had been under the surveillance of the
Diamond Fields police for suspected infractions of the illicit
Diamond Buying Act, colloquially known as IDB. Under
this local Act arrest is lawful on much slighter evidence than
would justify such a course elsewhere, but the police had
little to work upon until some purloined stones were actually
traced to Thomas just after he disappeared; the ordinary law
was thereupon invoked by the police, and a warrant was
granted for his apprehension.

The fugitive had a good start, and although traced to
Cape Town, he never lost the advantage he had gained, but
managed to escape on the outgoing liner *Grantully Castle*,
and the police feeling certain of his arrest at Southampton
telegraphed full particulars to England. Thomas would
appear to be well served by confederates for, when the
Grantully Castle arrived at Madeira, a telegram awaited him
and he suddenly left the ship, alleging urgent business at
Funchal, and stating his intention of coming on by the next
boat.

When the next liner duly arrived at Southampton it
brought an inspector of the Diamond Fields Police armed
with the warrant for Thomas' arrest, but no one on whom to
execute it. As usual, Thomas was a day ahead of his pursuers,
and for a time no trace of him could be found. At length,
through the *Castle* agent at Funchal, it was discovered that
Thomas had remained but a day or two there, having taken

passage for London in the *Bittern*, a cargo steamer trading to the Gold Coast.

The scene now changes to the Downs, where the inspector, in company with a London detective, awaited the *Bittern*. A slow sailer, she was believed to have encountered bad weather in the Bay of Biscay, and it was not until yesterday morning that she made her number off Deal, and was promptly boarded by the police in a pilot boat; but once again they were just too late.

Off the South Foreland a "hoveller" had tried to sell the *Bittern* some vegetables but instead secured a passenger in the person of Thomas, who struck a bargain with him, and was rowed ashore near Kingsdown. From there he appears to have walked to Walmer taking the train to Dover, where for the present he has been lost.

Thomas is stated to be a native of Colchester, for many years in Africa, and is described as a strongly built man of about forty, wearing a dark beard and moustache, and with a scar over the right brow caused by a dynamite explosion which blinded the eye.

Here was matter for reflection with a vengeance. As Pringle refilled his lamp and kindled the charred wick, his one thought was the possible identity of the cyclist with the man Thomas. The descriptions given in the *Chronicle* were inconclusive, but the cyclist had a very effective mask of dust and mud. True, he was beardless, but would not a shave be the first act of Thomas on arriving at Dover?

To Pringle it seemed such an obvious precaution that he dismissed the fact as irrelevant. The time, too, was sufficient for even an inexperienced rider to have cycled the distance. It was certainly a clever idea, and very characteristic of the man, to come by road rather than by the train with its scheduled times and its frequent stoppages, to say nothing of the telegraph wires running alongside.

As Pringle had almost conclusively proved, he had travelled up from the south by way of Tonbridge, yet he had shown an extreme desire to conceal the fact. Then, again, he talked of coming by the Colchester road, and Thomas was said to be a native of Colchester. It was a small matter, no doubt; but the fugitive, anxious to hide his tracks, would be sure to speak of a neighbourhood he knew – or, rather, which he thought he knew, for it was clear that Thomas, if it were he, had forgotten the main features of the route.

But supposing Thomas to have been the cyclist, where were the diamonds? Surely, thought Pringle, he must have some with him. And at the thought of the treasure to which he had been so near his pulse quickened. Could Thomas have concealed it about his person? Hardly, in view of his possible capture. But what of the cycle? He had shown considerable solicitude for the machine – in fact, he had scarcely loosened his hold on it. And had not he, Romney Pringle, tested the possibilities of a cycle for concealing jewellery? Smiling at the recollection he sat down to his breakfast.

About nine o'clock Pringle started in search of his new acquaintance, but at the hotel he was met by a fresh difficulty – he knew no name by which to describe the stranger, and could only ask for "a gentleman with a bicycle".

"You may well say the gentleman with the bicycle," exclaimed the waiter as he took Pringle's judicious tip. "That's what we all call him. Why, he wouldn't let us put it in the yard last night, but he stuck to it like cobbler's wax, and stood it in the passage, where he could see it all the time he was eating. An' would you believe it, sir?" – sinking his voice to a confidential whisper – "he actually took the machine up to his bedroom with him at night!"

Pringle having expressed his horror at this violation of decency, the waiter continued –

"Ah! And when the guv'nor heard of it and went up to speak to him about it, he'd locked the door and pretended not to hear. He said it was a valuable machine, but I've got a brother in the trade and I know something about machines myself, and I don't see it's anything out of the way."

"What name did he give?"

"Think it was Snaky, or something foreign like that." The waiter consulted a slate. "Ah! here it is, sir – 'Snaburgh, No. 24; call 7:30.' "

"Has he gone, then?" inquired Pringle anxiously.

"Took his machine out with him soon after eight. The guv'nor objected to his going out before he'd paid his bill, seeing as he'd got no luggage, so he paid up, and then took a look at the timetable, and asked when lunch was on."

"What timetable was it?"

" 'ABC' I saw him with."

"Do you expect him back?"

"Can't say for – why, dash my wig, here he is, cycle an' all!"

The cyclist, holding a small black bag and wheeling the machine, wormed his way into the lobby resolutely declining the waiter's assistance. On seeing Pringle he started, then paused, and half turned back, but encumbered as he was his movements were necessarily slow, and Pringle, ignoring the action, advanced with his most engaging smile.

"I'm so pleased to find you're none the worse for your accident. Allow me!" he steadied the machine against the wall. "Have you been for a morning ride?"

"Only to do some shopping," was the ungracious reply.

Mr Snaburgh, as he called himself, looked all the better for his morning toilet, and Pringle watched him closely in the endeavour to compare him with the rather vague newspaper description. He was certainly thick-set, and might have been any age from thirty to five-and-forty. His moustache was coal-black and drooped in cavalry fashion over his mouth; the chin had already grown a short stubble, and two fresh cuts upon his chops were eloquent of the hasty removal of a recent beard. There was a constant nervous twitching about the eyelids, but although shaded by the peak of the cap, a dirty-coloured corrugation over the right brow was quite apparent.

Pringle took special note of the right pupil. As Snaburgh stood he was in a full light, but yet it was unduly dilated, thus showing its insensibility to the light and the blindness of the eye.

"I must apologize for intruding on you so early in the day," said Pringle with all his wonted suaveness; "but a sprain is often at its worst a few hours after the accident."

"It's all right, thanks," gruffly.

"If I can be of any service to you while you're in town —"

"I'm not going to stay in town! Er — good morning!" And he resumed his elephantine struggle through the hall.

In face of this snub Pringle could do nothing, and fearful of rousing suspicions which might scare the fugitive into another sudden disappearance, he accepted the dismissal. As he passed out he overheard, "Shall I take the machine, sir?" and the reply, "No, I want a private sitting room where I can take it."

Pringle meditated upon two facts as he turned homeward. He had ascertained beyond any reasonable doubt that the cyclist was Thomas, and that the machine was as much as ever the object of his idolatry. The extraordinary pains to keep it in sight, his refusal to part with it even in his bedroom, the saddling himself with it when, as he said, he only went shopping, all pointed to the fact that a machine intrinsically worth some three or four pounds had a very special value in his eyes.

One thing was a little puzzling to Pringle: the man had no luggage — not even a cycle valise — the night before, yet at an early hour, almost before the shops were open, in fact, he had gone out and purchased a bag. Did he suspect how much comment his care of the cycle was arousing? Was he about to transfer its freight to the bag? Here again he displayed his usual shrewdness, for the "ABC" gave no hint as to the line he favoured.

Pringle wondered how much longer Thomas would remain at the hotel. He had certainly made inquiries about lunch, and the unloading of the cycle would take a little time. But then there was that story in the *Chronicle* to be reckoned with. Were Thomas to see that he would be sure to connect it with Pringle's visit, and would promptly vanish. But was it in any other paper? Pringle made a large investment in the journalism of the morning and, mounting an omnibus, industriously skimmed the whole. The *Chronicle* alone printed it, and he decided to take the risk of Thomas reading it there.

Hard by Furnival's Inn is an emporium where the appliances of every known sport (and even of a few unknown ones) are obtainable. Pringle was no stranger to the establishment, and making his way to the athletic department, purchased a cheap cycling suit and sweater, with a cap which he ornamented with an aggressive badge. Downstairs among the cycling accessories he brought a "ram's-horn" handlebar, and hurried back laden to his chambers.

His first step was to remove the characteristic port-wine mark on his right cheek with spirit, and then having blackened his fair hair and brows, he created the incipience of a moustache with the shreds from a camel-hair brush.

Although it would have been difficult for Pringle to look other than a gentleman, with his slim athletic figure clothed in the sweater, the cycling suit, and the cap and badge (especially the badge), he presented a fair likeness of the average Sunday scorcher. The manners of the tribe he fortunately saw no necessity to assume. To perfect the resemblance, the scorcher being comparable to a man who shall select a racehorse for a day's ride over country roads, it was necessary to "strip" his machine, so removing the mudguards and brake, and robbing the chain of its decent gear-case, he substituted the "ram's-horn" for his handlebar.

Towards noon Pringle rode down Arundel Street and, alighting at a tavern commanding a view of the Embankment Hotel, sat down to wait in the company of a beer-tankard: but as he slowly sipped the beer, his vigil unrewarded and the barman beginning to stare inquisitively, the thought arose again and again that Thomas had given him the slip.

He almost decided on the desperate step of visiting the hotel and once more pumping the friendly waiter, when, shortly after one, he caught a momentary glimpse of a familiar face as its owner examined the street over the coffee-room blinds.

Pringle drew a long breath. He was on the right scent, after all: and ordering a cut from the joint he made a hearty lunch preserving an unabated watch upon the hotel door. This was a somewhat irritating task. It was the autumn season, and with a full complement of country and American cousins in the house, there was a constant movement to and fro.

Nevertheless, his persistence was rewarded after an hour by a slight but portentous occurrence: a waiter emerged with a cycle, which he propped against the curb. It was the hired crock. By this time Pringle could have identified it among some thousands at a cycle show. But the owner? Where was he? What, Pringle asked himself, could have soured his affection for the machine? What else but the removal of the treasure?

Pringle was saved further speculation by the appearance of Thomas himself. He was carrying the handbag, and entered on an earnest conversation with the waiter, the subject of discussion appearing to be the cycle itself. Presently the waiter opened the toolbag, and, taking a wrench form it, commenced to adjust the handlebar, which Pringle for the first time noticed was all askew. This took some little time, and when the man finished he pointed to the saddle as if that too required attention, an office which he straightway performed. And all the while Thomas, with the bag fast held, contented himself with supervising the task.

The sight was an instructive one for Pringle. The disarrangement of the cycle was an assurance that the contents had been transferred, and Thomas clearly regarded the machine but as a means of locomotion.

Resisting the waiter's attempt to hold the bag while he mounted, Thomas scrambled to the saddle and steered a serpentine course up the slope, the bag bouncing and trembling in his grasp. Even had he been capable of the feat of turning round, he would have felt no apprehension of the youth who followed at a pace regulated by his own.

In the case of every pastime some special Providence would seem to direct the novice: either he has an impregnable run of luck, or he performs feats which he can never after attain. So it was with Thomas.

An indifferent rider, he boldly plunged into the torrent which roared along Fleet Street: unscathed he shot the rapids of Ludgate Circus, and kept a straight and fearless course onwards up the hill. But in Queen Victoria Street the steering became too complicated and, forced to dismount, he pushed the cycle for the remainder of the way.

Pringle had followed in some alarm that they might be hopelessly separated in the traffic, and more than once had even entertained ideas of seizing the bag in the midst of a purposed collision and trusting to luck to dodge into safety between the omnibuses. But he dismissed them all as crude and dangerous; besides, his artistic ideals revolted at the clumsiness of leaving any details to mere luck.

The pursuit led on through the City till presently Pringle found himself descending the approach to the Great Eastern terminus. Inside all was bustle and confusion, and they had to elbow an arduous track through the crowd. Seeing wisdom in a less intimate attendance, Pringle withdrew to the shelter of a flight of steps, and while Thomas perspired he rested. But he never relaxed his watch, and the moment the other emerged from the booking office and panted toward the labelling rack, Pringle followed on. As Thomas moved off with his machine Pringle palmed a shilling on the porter with the demand, "Same, please," and a few seconds later drew aside to read the label pasted on his spokes. It was *Witham*.

Handing the cycle to a porter he rushed to the booking office then on to the platform as the crock, in the indifferent absence of Thomas, was trundled into the van with customary official brutality; his own followed with a shade more consideration, and under the pretence of adjusting it he presently got into the van, and as he passed Thomas' machine buried a knife-blade in each of its tyres. He had just time to take his seat before the whistle sounded, and the train glided out of the station.

Witham was a good forty minutes off, and at every halt Pringle's shoulders blocked the carriage window. He feared lest Thomas should repeat his favourite strategy of alighting before his destination. But so long as they were in motion Pringle whiled the time by imagining fresh reasons for this mysterious journey.

He was staring at the map of the Great Eastern system which oppositely hung in the compartment, when his eye fell on a miniature steamboat voyaging a mathematically straight line drawn across from Harwich to the Hook of Holland. The figure suggested a new idea. Supposing the present trip had been arranged with an accomplice – could it in brief be a clever scheme to dispose of the diamonds in the best market? When more likely to disarm suspicion than for Thomas to cycle from Witham to Harwich?

"Witham!"

Pringle, with every sense alert, looked out. No one alighting? Yes, here he was. The guard had already evicted the two cycles when Thomas, with the precious valise, hurried down the platform and seized his own. The supreme moment had arrived.

Pringle waited until the other had disappeared, and stepped on to the platform as the train began to move. There was no need for him to hurry; the damage he had inflicted on the crock would ensure its leisurely running. And true enough, when he reached the station door Thomas had got but a little way along the road in a bumpy fashion, which even to his inexperience might have told the rapid deflation of the tyres. His progress was further complicated by the presence of the bag, which he had no means of fastening to the cycle; and, slowly as Pringle followed, the distance betweeen them rapidly shortened, until when Thomas turned into the main road he was nearly up to him.

Pringle halted a few seconds to allow a diplomatic gap to intervene, and then followed round the corner as Thomas shaped a painful course along the Colchester road. On and on, growing ever slower, the way led between high hedges, until with a pair of absolutely flat tyres there dawned upon Thomas' intelligence a suspicion that all was not well with the machine, and, dismounting, he leant it against the hedge.

"Can I lend you a repair? You seem badly punctured," piped Pringle in a high falsetto. He had shot by, and now, wheeling round, passed a little to the rear and propped his machine against a gate.

"I thought that was it. I haven't got a repair," was the least bearish reply that Pringle had yet heard from Thomas.

"You must get both tyres off – like this!" Pringle inverted the crock, and with the dexterity of long practice, ran his fingers round the rims and unnecessarily dragged out both the inner tubes for their entire length. "Catch hold for a second, will you, while I look for a patch."

Thomas innocently laid the bag at his feet and steadied the machine, when a violent thrust sent him diving headlong through the frame. With a spasm of his powerful back muscles he saved a sprawl into the hedge, and was on his feet in another second.

Pringle, the bag in hand, was already a dozen yards away. He had noted a fault in the hedge, and for this he made with all imaginable speed. The road sank just here, but scrambling cat-like up the bank, with a rending and tearing of his clothes, his bleeding hands forced a passage through the gap. Once clear of it he doubled back inside the hedge; beyond the gate there stood his cycle, and even as he neared it there was a scream of curses as the thorns waylaid Thomas in the gap.

In a bound Pringle was over the gate. The bag was hooked fast upon a staple; desperately he tugged, but the iron held until at a more violent wrench the leather ripped open. He seized the canvas packet within; it crisped in his fingers.

Behind there was a furious panting; he could almost feel the hot breaths, but as Thomas clutched the empty bag and collapsed across the gate, Pringle disappeared toward Colchester in a whirlwind of dust.

The Silkworms of Florence

"And this is all that is left of Brede now." The old beadle withdrew his hand, and the skull, with a rattle as of an empty wooden box, fell in its iron cage again.

"How old do you say it is?" asked Mr Pringle.

"Let me see," reflected the beadle, stroking his long grey beard. "He killed Mr Grebble in 1742, I think it was – the date's on the tombstone over yonder in the church – and he hung in these irons a matter of sixty or seventy year. I don't rightly know the spot where the gibbet stood, but it was in a field they used to call in my young days 'Gibbet Marsh.' You'll find it round by the Tillingham, back of the windmill."

"And is this the gibbet? How dreadful!" chorused the two daughters of a clergyman, very summery, very gushing, and very inquisitive, who with their father completed the party.

"Lor, no, miss! Why, that's the Rye pillory. It's stood up here nigh a hundred year! And now I'll show you the town charters." And the beadle, with some senile hesitation of gait, led the way into a small attic.

Mr Pringle's mythical literary agency being able to take care of itself, his chambers in Furnival's Inn had not seen him for a month past. To a man of his cultured and fastidious bent the Bank Holiday resort was especially odious; he affected regions unknown to the tripper, and his presence at Rye had been determined by Jeakes' quaint "Perambulation of the Cinque Ports", which he had lately picked up in Booksellers' Row.

Wandering with his camera from one decayed city to another, he had left Rye only to hasten back when disgusted with the modernity of the other ports, and for the last fortnight his tall slim figure had haunted the town, his fair complexion swarthy and his port-wine mark almost lost in the tanning begotten of the marsh winds and the sun.

"The town's had a rare lot of charters and privileges granted to it," boasted the beadle, turning to a chest on which for all its cobwebs and mildew the lines of elaborate carving showed distinctly. Opening it, he began to dredge up parchments from the huddled mass inside, giving very free translations of the old Norman-French or Latin the while.

"Musty, dirty old things!" was the comment of the two ladies.

Pringle turned to a smaller chest standing neglected in a dark corner, whose lid, when he tried it, he found also unlocked, and which was nearly as full of papers as the larger one.

"Are these town records also?" inquired Pringle, as the beadle gathered up his robes preparatory to moving on.

"Not they," was the contemptuous reply.

"That there chest was found in the attic of an old house that's just been pulled down to build the noo bank, and it's offered to the Corporation; but I don't think they'll spend money on rubbish like that!"

"Here's something with a big seal!" exclaimed the clergyman, pouncing on a discoloured parchment with the avid interest of an antiquary. The folds were glued with damp, and endeavouring to smooth them out the parchment slipped through his fingers; it dropped plumb by the weight of its heavy seal, and as he sprang to save it his glasses fell off and buried themselves among the papers. While he hunted for them Pringle picked up the document, and began to read.

"Not much account I should say," commented the beadle, with a supercilious snort.

"Ah! You should have seen our Jubilee Address, with the town seal to it, all in blue and red and gold – cost every penny of fifty pound! That's the noo bank what you're looking at from this window. How the town is improving, to be sure!" He indicated a nightmare in red brick and stucco which had displaced a Jacobean mansion.

And while the beadle prosed Pringle read:

CINQUE   TO ALL and every the Barons Bailiffs Jurats
PORTS   and Commonalty of the Cinque Port of Rye and
TO WIT   to Anthony Shipperbolt Mayor thereof:

WHEREAS it hath been adjudged by the Commission appointed under His Majesty's sign-manual of date March the twenty-third one thousand eight hundred and five that Anthony Shipperbolt Mayor of Rye hath been guilty of conduct unbefitting his office as a magistrate of the Cinque Ports and hath acted traitorously enviously and contrary to the love and affection his duty towards His Most Sacred Majesty and the good order of this Realm TO WIT that the said Anthony Shipperbolt hath accepted bribes from the enemies of His Majesty hath consorted with the same and did plot compass and go about to assist a certain prisoner of war the same being his proper ward and charge to escape from lawful custody NOW I William Pitt Lord Warden of the Cinque Ports do order and command you the said Anthony Shipperbolt and you are hereby required to forfeit and pay the sum of ten thousand pounds sterling into His Majesty's Treasury AND as immediate officer of His Majesty and by virtue and authority of each and every the ancient charters of the Cinque Ports I order and command you the said Anthony Shipperbolt to forthwith determine and refrain and you are hereby inhibited from exercising the office and dignity of Mayor of the said Cinque Port of Rye Speaker of the Cinque Ports Summoner of Brotherhood and Guestling and all and singular the liberties freedoms licenses exemptions and jurisdictions of Stallage Pontage Panage Keyage Murage Piccage Passage Groundage Scutage and all other powers franchises and authorities appertaining thereunto AND I further order and command you the said Anthony Shipperbolt to render to me within seven day s of the date hereof a full and true account of all monies fines amercements redemptions issues forfeitures tallies seals records lands messuages and hereditaments whatsoever and wheresoever that you hold have present custody of or have at any tie received in trust for the said Cinque Port of Rye wherein fail not at your peril. AND I further order and command you the said Barons Bailiffs Jurats and Commonalty of the said Cinque Port of Rye that you straitway meet and choose some true and loyal subject of His Majesty the same being of your number as fitting to hold the said office of Mayor of the said Cinque Port whose name you shall submit to my pleasure as soon as may be FOR ALL which this shall be your sufficient authority. Given at Downing Street this sixteenth day of May in the year of our Lord one thousand eight hundred and five.

GOD SAVE THE KING

The last two or three inches of the parchment were folded down, and seemed to have firmly adhered to the back – probably through the accidental running of the seal in hot weather. But the fall had broken the wax, and Pringle was now able to open the sheet to the full, disclosing some lines of script, faded and tremulously scrawled, it is true, but yet easy to be read:

"To my son, – Seek for the silkworms of Florence in Gibbet Marsh

Church Spire SE x S, Winchelsea Mill SW$\frac{1}{2}$W. AS."

Pringle read this curious endorsement more than once, but could make no sense of it. Concluding it was of the nature of a cypher, he made a note of it in his pocketbook with the idea of attempting a solution in the evening – a time which he found it difficult to get through, Rye chiefly depending for its attractions on its natural advantages.

By this time the clergyman had recovered his glasses, and, handing the document back to him, Pringle joined the party by the window. The banalities of the bank and other municipal improvements being exhausted, and the ladies openly yawning, the beadle proposed to show them what he evidently regarded as the chief glory of the Town Hall of Rye. The inquisitive clergyman was left studying the parchment, while the rest of the party adjourned to the council chamber. Here the guide proudly indicated the list of mayors, whose names were emblazoned on the chocolate-coloured walls to a length rivalling that of the dynasties of Egypt.

"What does this mean?" inquired Pringle. He pointed to the year 1805, where the name "Anthony Shipperbolt" appeared bracketed with another.

"That means he died during his year of office," promptly asserted the old man. He seemed never at a loss for an answer, although Pringle began to suspect that the prompter the reply the more inaccurate was it likely to be.

"Oh, what a smell of burning!" interrupted one of the ladies.

"And where's papa?" screamed the other.

"He'll be burnt to death."

There was certainly a smell of burning, which, being of a strong and pungent nature, perhaps suggested to the excited imagination of the ladies the idea of a clergyman on fire.

Pringle gallantly raced up the stairs. The fumes issued from a smouldering mass upon the floor, and beside it lay something which burnt with pyrotechnic sputtering; but neither bore any relation to the divine. He, though well representing what Gibbon has styled "the fat slumbers of the Church", was hopping about the miniature bonfire, now sucking his fingers and anon shaking them in the air as one in great agony.

Intuitively Pringle understood what had happened, and with a bound he stamped the smouldering parchment into unrecognizable tinder, and smothering the more viciously burning seal with his handkerchief he pocketed it as the beadle wheezed into the room behind the ladies, who were too concerned for their father's safety to notice the action.

"What's all this?" demanded the beadle, and glared through his spectacles.

"I've dr-r-r-opped some wa-wa-wa-wax – oh! – upon my hand!"

"Waxo?" echoed the beadle, sniffing suspiciously.

"He means a wax match, I think," Pringle interposed chivalrously. The parchment was completely done for, and he saw no wisdom in advertising the fact.

"I'll trouble you for your name and address," insisted the beadle in all the pride of office.

"What for?" the incendiary objected.

"To report the matter to the Fire Committee."

"Very well, then – Cornelius Hardgiblet, rector of Logdown," was the impressive reply; and tenderly escorted by his daughters the rector departed with such dignity as an occasional hop, when his fingers smarted a little more acutely, would allow him to assume.

It still wanted an hour or two to dinner time as Pringle unlocked the little studio he rented on the Winchelsea road. Originally an office, he had made it convertible into a very fair darkroom, and here he was accustomed to spend his afternoons in developing the morning's photographs. But photography had little interest for him today. Ever since Mr Hardgiblet's destruction of the document – which, he felt certain, was no accident – Pringle had cast about for some motive for the act. What could it be but that the parchment contained a secret, which the rector, guessing, had wanted to keep to himself? He must look up the incident of the mayor's degradation. So sensational an event, even for such stirring days as those, would scarcely go unrecorded by local historians.

Pringle had several guidebooks at hand in the studio, but a careful search only disclosed that they were unanimously silent as to Mr Shipperbolt and his affairs. Later on, when returning, he had reason to bless his choice of an hotel. The books in the smoking room were not limited, as usual, to a few timetables and an ancient copy of Ruff's "Guide". On the contrary, Murray and Black were prominent and above all Hillpath's monumental "History of Rye", and in this last he found the information he sought. Said Hillpath:

> In 1805 Anthony Shipperbolt, then Mayor of Rye, was degraded from office, his property confiscated, and himself condemned to stand in the pillory with his face to the French coast, for having assisted Jules Florentin, a French prisoner of war, to escape from the Ypres Tower Prison.
>
> He was suspected of having connived at the escape of several other prisoners of distinction, presumably for reward. He had been a shipowner trading with France, and his legitimate trade suffering as a result of the war he had undoubtedly resorted to smuggling, a form of trading which, to the principals engaged in it at least, carried little disgrace with it, being winked at by even the most law-abiding persons.
>
> Shipperbolt did not long survive his degradation, and, his only son being killed soon after while resisting a revenue cutter when in charge of his father's vessel, the family became extinct.

Here, thought Pringle, was sufficient corroboration of the parchment. The details of the story were clear, and the only mysterious thing about it was the endorsement. His original idea of its being a cypher hardly squared with the simple address, "To my son," and the "AS" with which it concluded could only stand for the initials of the deposed mayor.

There was no mystery either about "Gibbet Marsh", which, according to the beadle's testimony, must have been a well-known spot a century ago, while the string of capitals he easily recognized as compass bearings. There only remained the curious expression, "The Silkworms of Florence," and that was certainly a puzzle. Silkworms are a product of Florence, he knew; but they were unlikely to be exported in such troublous times. And why were they deposited in such a place as Gibbet Marsh?

He turned for enlightenment to Hillpath, and poured over the passage again and again before he saw a glimmer of sense. Then suddenly he laughed, as the cypher resolved itself into a pun, and a feeble one at that.

While Hillpath named the prisoner as Florentine and more than hinted at payment for services rendered, the cypher indicated where Florentine products were to be found... Shipperbolt ruined, his property confiscated, what more likely than that he should conceal the price of his treason in Gibbet Marsh – a spot almost as shunned in daylight as in darkness? Curious as the choice of the parchment for such a purpose might be, the endorsement was practically a will. He had nothing else to leave.

Pringle was early afoot the next day. Gibbet Marsh has long been drained and its very name forgotten, but the useful Murray indicated its site clearly enough for him to identify it; and it was in the middle of a wide and lonely field, embanked against the winter inundations, that Pringle commenced to work out the bearings approximately with a pocket compass.

He soon fixed his starting point, the church tower dominating Rye from every point of view; but of Winchelsea there was nothing to be seen for the trees. Suddenly, just where the green mass thinned away to the northward, something rose and caught the sunbeams for a moment, again and still again, and with a steady gaze he made out the revolving sails of a windmill.

This was as far as he cared to go for the moment; without a good compass and a sounding-spud it would be a dire waste of time to attempt to fix the spot. He walked across the field, and was in the very act of mounting the stile when he noticed a dark object, which seemed to skim in jerky progression along the top of the embankment. While he looked the thing enlarged, and as the path behind the bank rose uplifted itself into the head, shoulders, and finally the entire person of the rector of Logdown. He had managed to locate Gibbet Marsh, it appeared; but, as he stepped into the field and wandered aimlessly about, Pringle judged that he was still a long way from penetrating the retreat of the silkworms.

Among the passengers by the last train down from London that night was Pringle. He carried a cricketing-bag, and when safely inside the studio he unpacked first a sailor's jersey, peaked cap and trousers, then a small but powerful spade, a very neat portable pick, a few fathoms of Manila rope, several short lengths of steel rod (each having a screw-head, by which they united into a single long one), and finally a three-inch prismatic compass.

Before sunrise the next morning Pringle started out to commence operations in deadly earnest, carrying his jointed rods as a walking stick, while his coat bulged with the prismatic compass. The town, a victim to the enervating influence of the visitors, still slumbered, and he had to unbar the door of the hotel himself. He did not propose to do more than locate the exact spot of the treasure; indeed he felt that to do even that would be a good morning's work.

On the way down in the train he had taken a few experimental bearings from the carriage window, and felt satisfied with his own dexterity. Nevertheless, he had a constant dread lest the points given should prove inaccurate. He felt dissatisfied with the Winchelsea bearing. For aught he knew, not a single tree that now obscured the view might have been planted; the present mill, perhaps, had not existed; or even another might have been visible from the marsh. What might not happen in the course of nearly a century?

He had already made a little calculation, for a prismatic compass being graduated in degrees (unlike the mariner's, which has but thiryt-two points), it was necessary to reduce the bearings to degrees, and this had been the result:

Rye Church spire SE x S = 146° 15'.
Winchelsea Mill SW^1/2 W = 230° 37'.

When he reached the field not a soul was anywhere to be seen; a few sheep browsed here and there, and high overhead a lark was singing. At once he took a bearing from the church spire. He was a little time in getting the right pointing; he had to move step by step to the right, continuing to take observations, until at last the church weathercock bore truly 146 $1/4$° through the sightvane of the compass.

Turning half round, he took an observation of the distant mill. He was a long way out this time; so carefully preserving his relative position to the church, he backed away, taking alternate observations of either object until both spire and mill bore in the right directions.

The point where the two bearings intersected was some fifty yards form the brink of the Tillingham, and, marking the spot with his compass, Pringle began to probe the earth in a widening circle, first with one section of his rod, then, with another joint screwed to it, and finally with a length of three, so that the combination reached to a depth of eight feet. He had probed every square inch of a circle described perhaps twenty feet from the compass, when he suddenly stumbled upon a loose sod, nearly impaling himself upon the sounding-rod; and before he could rise his feet, sliding and slipping, had scraped up quite a large surface of turf, as did his hand, in each case disclosing the fat, brown alluvium beneath.

A curious fact was that the turf had not been cut in regular strips, as if for removal to some garden; neatly as it was relaid, it had been lifted in shapeless patches, some large, some small, while the solid underneath was all soft and crumbling, as if that too had been recently disturbed. Someone had been before him!

Cramped and crippled by his prolonged stooping, Pringle stretched himself at length upon the turf. As he lay and listened to the song that trilled from the tiny speck just visible against a woolly cloud, he felt that it was useless to search further. That a treasure had once been hidden thereabouts he felt convinced, for anything but specie would have been useless at such an unsettled time for commercial credit, and would doubtless have been declined by Shipperbolt; but whatever form the treasure had taken, clearly it was no longer present.

The sounds of toil increased around. Already a barge was on its way up the muddy stream; at any moment he might be the subject of gaping curiosity. He carefully replaced the turfs, wondering the while who could have anticipated him, and what find, if any, had rewarded the searcher.

Thinking it best not to return by the nearest path, he crossed the river some distance up, and taking a wide sweep halted on Cadborough Hill to enjoy for the hundredth time the sight of the glowing roofs, huddled tier after tier upon the rock, itself rising sheer from the plain; and far and beyond, and snowed all over with grazing flocks, the boundless green of the seaward marsh.

Inland, the view was only less extensive, and with some ill humour he was eyeing the scene of his fruitless labour when he observed a figure moving about Gibbet Marsh. At such a distance it was hard to see exactly what was taking place, but the action of the figure was so eccentric that, with a quick suspicion as to its identity, Pringle laid his traps upon the ground and examined it through his pocket telescope.

It was indeed Mr Hardgiblet. But the new feature in the case was that the rector appeared to be taking a bearing with a compass, and although he returned over and over again to a particular spot (which Pringle recognized as the same over which he himself had spent the early morning hours), Mr Hardgiblet repeatedly shifted his ground to the right, to the left, and round about, as if dissatisfied with his observations.

There was only one possible explanation of all this. Cleverer than Pringle had thought him, the rector must have hit upon the place indicated in the parchment, his hand must have removed the turf, and he it was who had examined the soil beneath.

Not for the first time in his life, Pringle was disagreeably reminded of the folly of despising an antagonist, however contemptible he may appear. But at least he had one consolation; the rector's return and his continued observations showed that he had been no more successful in his quest than was Pringle himself. The silkworms were still unearthed.

The road down from Cadborough is long and dusty, and, what with the stiffness of his limbs and the thought of his wasted morning, Pringle, when he reached his studio and took the compass from his pocket, almost felt inclined to fling it through the open window into the "cut". But the spasm of irritability passed. He began to accuse himself of making some initial error in the calculations, and carefully went over them again – with an identical result.

Now that Mr Hardgiblet was clearly innocent of its removal, he even began to doubt the existence of the treasure. Was it not incredible, he asked himself, that for nearly a century it should have remained hidden? As to its secret (a punning endorsement on an old parchment), was it not just as open to any other investigator in all the long years that had elapsed? Besides, Shipperbolt might have removed the treasure himself in alarm for its safety.

The thought of Shipperbolt suggested a new idea. Instruments of precision were unknown in those days – supposing Shipperbolt's compass had been inaccurate? He took down Norie's "Navigation", and ran throughout the chapter on the compass. There was a section headed "Variation and how to apply it", which he skimmed through, considering that the question did not arise, when, carelessly reading on, his attention was suddenly arrested by a table of "Changes in variation from year to year".

Running his eye down this he made the startling discovery that, whereas the variation at that moment was about $16°$ $31'$ west, in 1805 it was no less than $24°$. Here was indeed a wide margin for error. All the time he was searching for the treasure it was probably lying right at the other side of the field!

At once he started to make a rough calculation, determined that it should be a correct one this time. As the variation of 1805 and that of the moment showed a difference of 7° 29', to obtain the true bearing it was necessary for him to subtract this difference from Shipperbolt's points, thus:

Rye Church spire SE x S = 146° 15',
deduct 7° 29' = 138° 46'.
Winchelsea Mill SW$^{1}/2$ W = 230° 37',
deduct 7° 29' = 223° 8'.

The question of the moment concerned his next step. Up to the present Mr Hardgiblet appeared unaware of the error. But how long, thought Pringle, would he remain so? Any work on navigation would set him right, and as he seemed keenly on the scent of the treasure he was unlikely to submit to a check of this nature. Like Pringle, too, he seemed to prefer the early morning hours for his researches. Clearly there was no time to lose.

On his way up to lunch Pringle remarked that the whole town was agog. Crowds were pouring in from the railway station; at every corner strangers were inquiring their road; the shops were either closed or closing; a stream roundabout hooted in the cricket field. The holiday aspect of things was marked by the display on all sides of uncomfortably best clothing worn with a reckless and determined air of Pleasure Seeking. Even the artists, the backbone of the place, had shared the excitement, or else, resenting the invasion of their pitches by the unaccustomed crowd, were sulking indoors. Anyhow, they had disappeared. Not until he reached the hotel and read on a poster the programme of the annual regatta to be held that day, did Pringle realize the meaning of it all.

In the course of lunch – which, owing to the general disorganization of things, was a somewhat scrambled meal – it occurred to him that here was his opportunity. The regatta was evidently the great event of the year; every idler would be drawn to it, and no worker who could be spared would be absent. The treasure-field would be even lonelier than in the days of Brede's gibbet. He would be able to locate the treasure that afternoon once for all; then, having marked the spot, he could return at night with his tools and remove it.

When Pringle started out the streets were vacant and quiet as on a Sunday, and he arrived at the studio to find the quay an idle waste and the shipping in the "cut" deserted. As to the meadow, when he got there, it was forsaken even by the sheep. He was soon at work with his prismatic compass, and after half an hour's steady labour he struck a spot about an eighth of a mile distant from the scene of his morning's failure.

Placing his compass as before at the point of intersection, he began a systematic puncturing of the earth around it. It was a wearisome task, and, warned by his paralysis of the morning, he rose every now and then to stretch and watch for possible intruders.

Hours seemed to have passed, when the rod encountered something hard. Leaving it in position, he probed all around with another joint, but there was no resistance even when he doubled its length, and his sense of touch assured him this hardness was merely a casual stone.

Doggedly he resumed his task until the steel jammed again with a contact less harsh and unyielding. Once more he left the rod touching the buried mass, and probed about, still meeting an obstruction. And then with widening aim he stabbed and stabbed, striking this new thing until he had roughly mapped a space some twelve by eight inches.

No stone was this, he felt assured; the margins were too abrupt, the corners too sharp, for aught but a chest. He rose exultingly. Here beneath his feet were the silkworms of Florence. The secret was his alone. But it was growing late; the afternoon had almost merged into evening, and far away across the field stretched his shadow.

Leaving the sounding-rod buried with the cord attached, he walked toward a hurdle on the river bank, paying out the cord as he went, and hunted for a large tone. This found, he tied a knot in the cord to mark where the hurdle stood, and following it back along the grass pulled up the rod and pressed the stone upon the loosened earth in its place. Last of all, he wound the cord upon the rod. His task would be an easy one again. All he need do was to find the knot, tie the cord at that point to the hurdle, start off with the rod in hand, and when all the cord had run off search for the stone to right or left of the spot he would find himself standing on.

As he re-entered the town groups of people were returning from the regatta – the seafaring to end the day in the abounding taverns, the staider on their way to the open-air concert, the cinematograph, and the fireworks, which were to brim the cup of their dissipation.

Pringle dined early, and then made his way to the concert field, and spent a couple of hours in studying the natured history of the Ryer. The fireworks were announced for nine, and as the hour approached the excitement grew and the audience swelled. When a fairly accurate census of Rye might have been taken in the field, Pringle edged through the crowd and hurried along the deserted streets to the studio.

To change his golf suit for the sea-clothing he had brought from town was the work of a very few minutes, and the port-wine mark never resisted the smart application of a little spirit. Then, packing the sounding-rod and cord in the cricketing bag, along with the spade, pick, and rope, he locked the door, and stepped briskly out along the solitary road.

From the little taverns clinging to the rock opposite came roars of discordant song, for while the losers in the regatta sought consolation, the winners paid the score, and all grew steadily drunk together.

He lingered a moment on the sluice to watch the tide as it poured impetuously up from the lower river. A rocket whizzed, and as it burst high over the town a roar of delight was faintly borne across the marsh.

Although the night was cloudy and the moon was only revealed at long intervals, Pringle, with body bent, crept cautiously from bush to bush along the bank; his progress was slow, and the hurdle had been long in sight before he made out a black mass in the water below. At first he took it for the shadow of a bush that stood by, but as he came nearer it took the unwelcome shape of a boat with its painter fast to the hurdle; and throwing himself flat in the grass he writhed into the opportune shade of the bush.

It was several minutes before he ventured to raise his head and peer around, but the night was far too dark for him to see many yards in any direction – least of all towards the treasure. As he watched and waited he strove to imagine some reasonable explanation for the boat's appearance on the scene. At another part of the river he would have taken slight notice of it; but it was hard to see what anyone could want in the field at that hour, and the spot chosen for landing was suggestive.

What folly to have located the treasure so carefully! He must have been watched that afternoon; round the field were scores of places where a spy might conceal himself. Then, too, who could have taken such deep interest in his movements? Who but Mr Hardgiblet, indeed? This set him wondering how many had landed from the boat; but a glance showed that it carried only a single pair of sculls, and when he wriggled nearer he saw but three footprints upon the mud, as of one who had taken just so many steps across it.

The suspense was becoming intolerable. A crawl of fifty yards or so over damp grass was not to be lightly undertaken; but he was just on the point of coming out from the shadow of the bush, when a faint rhythmic sound arose, to be followed by a thud. He held his breath, but could hear nothing more. He counted up to a hundred – still silence. He rose to his knees, when the sound began again, and now it was louder. It ceased; again there was the thud, and then another interval of silence. Once more; it seemed quite close, grew louder, louder still, and resolved itself into the laboured breathing of a man who now came into view.

He was bending under a burden which he suddenly dropped, as if exhausted, and then, after resting awhile, slowly raised it to his shoulders and panted onwards, until, staggering beneath his load, he lurched against the hurdle, his foot slipped, and he rolled with a crash down the muddy bank. In that moment, Pringle recognized the more than usually unctuous figure of Mr Hardgiblet, who embraced a small oblong chest. Spluttering and fuming, the rector scrambled to his feet, and after an unsuccessful hoist or two, dragged the chest into the boat. Then, taking a pause for breath, he climbed the bank again and tramped across the field.

Mr Hardgiblet was scarcely beyond earshot when Pringle, seizing his bag, jumped down to the waterside. He untied the painter, and shoving off with his foot scrambled into the boat as it slid out on the river.

With a paddle of his hand alongside, he turned the head upstream, and then dropped his bag with all its contents overboard and crouched along the bottom.

A sharp cry rang out behind, and, gently, he peeped over the gunwale. There by the hurdle stood Mr Hardgiblet, staring thunderstruck at the vacancy. The next moment he caught sight of the strayed boat, and started to run after it; and as he ran with many a trip and stumble of wearied limbs, he gasped expressions which were not those of resignation to his mishap.

Meantime, Pringle, his face within a few inches of the little chest, sought for some means of escape. He had calculated on the current bearing him out of sight long before the rector could return, but such activity as this discounted all his plans. All at once he lost the sounds of pursuit, and raising his head, he saw that Mr Hardgiblet had been forced to make a detour around a little plantation which grew to the water's edge.

At the next sound, Pringle seized the sculls, and with a couple of long rapid strokes grounded the boat beneath a bush on the opposite bank. There he tumbled the chest on to the mud, and jumping after it shoved the boat off again. As it floated free and resumed its course upstream, Pringle shouldered the chest, climbed up the bank, and keeping in the shade of a hedge plodded heavily across the field.

Day was dawning as Pringle extinguished the lamp in his studio, and setting the shutters ajar allowed the light to fall upon the splinters, bristling like a cactus hedge, of what had been an oaken chest. The wood had proved hard as the iron which clamped and bound it, but scarcely darker or more begrimed than the heap of metal discs it had just disgorged. A few of these, fresh from a bath of weak acid, glowed golden as the sunlight, displaying indifferently a bust with "Bonaparte Premier Consul" surrounding it, or on the reverse "République Française, anno XI, 20 francs".

Such were the silkworms of Florence.

The Box of Specie

"Now then, sir, if you're coming!"

Mr Pringle, carrying a brown gladstone, was the last to cross the gangway before it was hauled back on to the landing stage. The steam ceased to roar from the escape pipes, impatiently tingled the bells in the engine room; then, pulsating to the rhythmic thud of her screws, the liner swung from the quay and silently picked her way down the crowded Pool. As reach succeeded reach the broadening stream opened a clearer course, and the *Mary Bland* moved to the full sweep of the ebbing tide; a whitened path began to lengthen in her wake, for nearing Tilbury the Thames becomes a clean and wholesome stream, and its foam is not as that of porter.

The day had been wet and gusty, and although, when he stepped aboard, the declining sun shown brightly, there was a touch of autumn rawness in the air which induced Pringle to seek a sheltered corner. Such he found by the break of the poop, and here he sat and watched the stowing of the cargo, the last arrival of which encumbered the after-deck.

By the time Tilbury was in sight all had been sent down the after-hatch but three small cases which the mate and purser, who stood superintending operations, appeared to view with a jealous eye. They were clamped with iron, of small size (about fourteen inches long by seven wide and four deep), and Pringle, even from where he sat, could read the direction in bold, black letters on the nearest:

THE MANAGER
Ivory and Produce Company
Cameroons

These were obviously for transshipment, since the *Mary Bland's* route was but London to Rotterdam. It was to Rotterdam that Pringle was bound. The journey was not undertaken for pleasure; he was en route for Amsterdam on business of peculiar interest, and not unconnected with precious stones, Amsterdam, as everybody knows, being the headquarters of the diamond-cutting industry. But this by the way.

The men were about attaching the chain tackle to the nearest of the three boxes when the captain came halfway down from the bridge.

"Haven't you got that specie stowed, Mr Trimble? It'll be dark presently." He addressed the mate with just a little anxiety in the tone.

"All right, sir," interposed the purser. "We just wanted to get the deck clear before I opened the strongroom."

"Go ahead, then," and the captain returned to the bridge.

The purser disappeared below, and presently came his voice from the after-hatch:

"Lower away, there!"

With much clanking and rattling of the chain, a case swung for a moment over the gulf, and then disappeared. A second followed, and a third was about to join them, when a voice from somewhere forward called:

"Steamer on the starboard bow!"

As the sun went down a grey mist, rising from the Cliffe marshes, had first blotted out the banks and then steamed across the fairway, which but a few minutes before had shown a clear course through the reach. It was quite local, and a big ocean tramp, coming slowly upstream, was just emerging from the obscurity as the *Mary Bland* encountered it.

"Hard a-starboard!" roared the captain, as he gave a sharp tug at the whistle lanyard. The man at the wheel spun it till the brasswork on the spokes seemed an endless golden ring. "Bang, clank! bang, clank!" went the steam steering-gear with a jarring tremor on deck, answered by the furious din of the engine-room telegraph as the captain jammed the indicator at "full speed astern". And on came the tramp showing bulkier through the mist.

"All hands forward with fenders!" and the men by the after-hatch scurried forward, the mate at their head. Slowly the vessels approached amid a whirr of bells and frantically shouted orders, their whistles hooting the regulation blasts. Suddenly, as but a few yards intervened, they obeyed their helms and slowly paid off, almost scraping one another's sides as they slid by, while at half-speed the *Mary Bland* plunged into the fog, her siren continuing the concert begun by the now silent tramp.

All at once there was a loud shout from the water, and a chocolate-coloured topsail, with a little dogvane above it, rose on the port bow. Once more the captain's hand wrenched the telegraph to "full speed astern", but it was too late. There was a concussion, plainly felt all over the steamer, a grinding and a splintering noise, and the topsail with its little weathercock dogvane had disappeared. The after-coming crowd rushed back again to find the *Mary Bland* drifting with the tide through an archipelago of hay trusses.

"Where in thunder are yer comin' to?" sounded in plaintive protest from the nearest truss. "Ain't there room enough roun' Coal-'ouse point for the likes of you?"

"What have we run down, Mr Trimble?" demanded the captain, his hands quivering on the bridge rail in a spasm of suppressed excitement.

"I think it's a hay barge, sir. It looks like a man floating on a truss over there on the port beam," said the mate, pointing in the direction of the voice.

"Get a boat out then, lively, and pick him up! And send that lookout man to me – I want to speak to him."

The men were already handling the falls, and, as the hapless lookout man slouched aft, the first officer, jumping into the boat with four sailors, was lowered to the water, and rowed towards the survivor of the barge.

All this time Pringle had remained near the after-hatch. When the collision seemed imminent he was about to follow the general movement to the centre of interest, when a light suddenly flashed on the port side, and, even as he gazed in wonder, ceased as abruptly as it rose. He stopped and looked about him; the gathering gloom of the evening seemed deeper after the momentary light, everyone was forward, the deck quite deserted, and the box of specie for the time ignored. Not altogether, though. A sailor was coming aft, detailed, no doubt, to watch the treasure where it lay.

Noting how stealthily he approached, Pringle drew back into his corner and watched him. The man walked on tiptoe, with every now and then a backward glance; and, for all the dimness of the fog and the oncoming night, he stalked along, taking advantage of every slightest shadow. Clearly he imagined that everyone was forward; he never gave a glance in Pringle's direction, but moved "the beard on the shoulder". On he stole till he reached the deserted box, and there he stopped and crouched down. Faint echoes were heard from forward, but not a soul came anywhere near the after-hatch. The captain was, of course, on the bridge; but, having relieved his feelings at the expense of the lookout man, was now absorbed in trying to follow the progress of the mate among the hay trusses.

Presently the light shot up again, and now a little closer. As it flickered and oscillated, Pringle saw that it came from a slender cylindrical lamp, supported by a sort of conical iron cage topping a large, black-coloured buoy, which floated some twenty feet off from the *Mary Bland*. The sight appeared to nerve the sailor to action; it seemed, indeed, as if he had waited for the buoy to reveal itself.

Dragging the box aside as gently as its weight allowed, he seized the chain placed ready for the tackle-hook, and tried to raise it. Again and again he made the attempt, but the weight seemed beyond his single strength. In the midst the light flared out once more; it was just opposite the ship, and as the buoy slowly dipped and turned, with a curtsey to this side and to that, the word "OVENS", in large white capitals, showed upon it before the light went out and all was dark again.

With a wrench and a groan, the man tilted the box on end; then, bracing himself, he raised it first to a bollard, and with a final and desperate heave to the gunwale. And then a curious thing happened. When presently the light shone the chest had disappeared, but, as if tracing its descent, the man hung over the side, his feet slipping and squirming to get a purchase, and as the light passed the sound of his struggling continued in the darkness.

At the next flash he was gone − all but a hand, which still gripped the gunwale, while his feet could be heard drumming furiously against the vessel's side; and now, as his fingers slipped from their agonizing hold, he gave a shriek for help, and then another and another.

Pringle darted across the deck, but the unfortunate wretch was beyond help; his hand wedged fast in the chain, he had been dragged overboard by the momentum of nearly a hundred weight of specie. And as he plunged headlong into the river the beacon shimmered upon the fountain of spray, a few jets even breaking in cascade against the sides of the buoy.

The cries of the drowning man had passed unnoticed. The boat had reached the barge just as the truss began to break up in the swirl; the passengers were cheering lustily, and Pringle walked quietly forward and mingled unperceived with the crowd. While rescued and rescuers climbed on board, the captain telegraphed "full speed ahead", and the *Mary Bland* resumed her voyage, so prolific of incident.

A group of passengers were discussing the proper course to have pursued had the collision with the tramp steamer actually occurred. A burly man with a catarrhal Teutonic accent maintained that the only sensible thing to do would have been to scramble on board the colliding ship. "At the worst," said he, "she would only have had two or three of her fore compartments stove in, whilst we stood to have a hole punched in our side big enough for an omnibus to drive through. We should have sunk inside of ten minutes, whilst they would have floated – well, long enough to have got us comfortably ashore."

In this discussion Pringle innocently joined, with an eye on the captain, who paced the ridge in ignorance of the new anxiety in store for him. Meanwhile, the purser had remained at his post in the strongroom. He awaited the further storage of the specie; but, although he could hear the men returning to the hatchway, not a shadow of the box appeared. At length he cried impatiently:

"Lower away, there – oh, lower away!"

"There ain't no more up 'ere, sir," said one of the men, as he put his head over the coaming.

"*No more!*" repeated the purser in hollow tones from the depths. "Send down that third box of specie – the money, I mean. Ah, you jackass! Don't stand grinning there! Where's the box you were going to send down when that cursed hooker nearly ran into us? Where's Mr Trimble?"

" 'E's with the captain, sir. Ain't the box down there? Didn't we send it down atop of the other two 'fore we went forward?"

Bang! went the strongroom door as the purser, without further discussion, rushed up on deck.

"Where's that third box of specie, Mr Trimble?"

The captain and the mate stared down at him from the bridge without answering.

"These idiots think they sent it down; but I have only received two, and it's nowhere about the deck."

The captain gasped and turned pale.

"When did you last see it?" he asked the mate.

"Just before we got into the fog."

The captain suppressed an oath.

"Go down with the purser, Mr Trimble, and see if it's fallen down the hatch."

Twenty minutes saw the mate return, hot and perspiring.

"Can't see a bit of it, sir," he reported; "and, what's more, Cogle seems to have disappeared as well!"

"Cogle?"

"Yes, sir. He was working the crane, but no one has seen him since. He can't have jumped overboard with the specie."

"Rot! Why, that box held five thousand sovereigns according to the manifest, and couldn't weigh an ounce less than three-quarters of a hundredweight altogether! You can't put a thing like that in your pocket, can you?"

The mate glanced doubtfully at the passengers on the saloon deck, but none showed such a bulging of the person as might be expected from a concealed box of specie.

"How would it be to put back to Gravesend and inform the police?" he suggested. "Cogle must have tumbled overboard in the ruction."

"It's no good putting back," the captain decided gloomily. "That specie was delivered right enough, and I'm responsible for it. It can't have fallen overboard, so it's on the ship somewhere – that I'll swear. Can't you suggest anything?" he added testily, as the mate continued to cast a suspicious eye on all around.

"Why not search the passengers' luggage?"

"Search your grandmother!" returned the captain contemptuously. "How can I do that? Hold on, though – I'll send you ashore as soon as we get to Rotterdam, and we'll ask the police to stand by while the Customs fellows search the luggage. Not a mother's son leaves this ship except the passengers; and as to the cargo, our agent'll see after that." And he went below to "log down" the events of the day whilst they were fresh in his memory.

The one person who could have thrown any light on the mystery remained silent. Pringle had resolved to be the dead man's legatee. It would be a large order, no doubt, to fish the chest up again, but the light marked a shoal thereabouts, and the depth was unlikely to be great; and, thinking the affair over, Pringle had little doubt that it was the sight of the buoy, a fixed watermark, which had determined the man to jettison the specie where he did.

As soon as he got back to London again, Pringle devoted some time to a careful study of Pearson's "Nautical Almanac." From this useful publication he learnt that at the time the *Mary Bland* was on her exciting course down the river it was the first of the ebb tide – that is to say, about three-quarters of an hour after high water. Now, inasmuch as a buoy is moored by a considerable length of chain, it is able to drift about within a circle of many feet; hence Pringle, to ensure success in his search, must choose a state of the tide identical with that prevailing when the box disappeared. At the same time, he proposed, for obvious reasons, to work at night, and preferably a moonless one.

At length he found that all these conditions were present about seven in the evening of the tenth day after his return.

Pringle, among his varied accomplishments, could handle a boat with most yachtsmen; and, leaving his chambers in Furnival's Inn for a season, he took up his residence at Erith. Here, attired in yachting costume, he spent depressing hours among the forlorn and aged craft at disposal, until, lighting on a boat suited to his purpose, he promptly hired it.

It was some eighteen feet long, half-decked, and carried standing lug and mizzen sails; but its chief attraction to Pringle was the presence of a small cabin in the forepeak, and to the door, as soon as he had taken possession, he fitted a hasp and staple, and secured it with a Yale padlock. His next thought was of the dredging tackle, and this he collected in the course of several trips to London. In the end, when the day of his enterprise dawned, two fathoms of chain, with half a dozen grapnels made fast to it, together with a twelve fathom rope and a spare block, were all stowed safely in the forepeak.

"Nice day for a sail, sir," remarked the boatkeeper, as Pringle walked along the landing stage soon after two o'clock in the afternoon.

"Yes; I want to take advantage of this north-west wind." And, getting into the boat, he was rowed towards the wooden railway pier, off which his boat lay.

"Well, I didn't think you were a gent to take advantage of anyone," chuckled the man. He had a green memory of certain judicious tips on Pringle's part, and he spoke with an eye to other layouts of a like kind. Pringle smiled obligingly at the witticism, and made a further exhibition of palm-oil as they reached the yacht. Scrambling aboard he cast loose, and, hoisting the mizzen, paddled out into the stream and set the mainsail.

The tide was running strong against him, but the wind blew fairly fresh from the north-west and helped him on a steady course down the river. The sail bellied and drew, while the intermittent cheep-cheep from the sheet-block was answered by the continuous musical tinkle under the forefoot.

By six o'clock Pringle had got out of the narrower reaches, and it was nearly dark as he passed Tilbury. A slight mist began to steal across from the marshes, but, with a natural desire to avoid observation, he showed no light. His course was now easier, for the tide began to turn; but although he kept an intent watch for the buoy it perversely hid itself. He was just about to tack and run upstream again, concluding that he must have passed the spot, when suddenly the occulting light glimmered through the mist on his port beam. Shooting up into the wind, he headed straight for the buoy, and as his bow almost touched it the light blazed clearly.

On the way down he had rigged up the spare block on the bumpkin about a foot beyond the stern, and through it rove his twelve-fathom rope, securing it by a turn round a cleat, the two-fathom chain with the grapnels fast on the other end. And now his real work began. He heaved the chain and grapnels overboard and began to tack to and fro and up and down upon the course he judged the *Mary Bland* had taken as she passed the buoy.

The night was chilly, and Pringle was proportionately ravenous of the cold-meat sandwiches he had stuffed into his pockets on starting – he knew better than to reduce his temperature by the illusory glow of alcohol.

It was very monotonous, this drifting with the stream and then tacking up against it, his cruising centred by the winking light; and every now and then he would shift his ground a few feet to port of starboard as the grapnel fruitlessly swept the muddy bottom.

Presently, while drifting downstream, the boat lost way, and looking over the stern he saw the rope taut as steel wire. The grapnel had caught, and in some excitement he hauled on the rope. As the hooks came in sight he saw by the intermittent flare that they were indeed fast to a chain – not the crossed chain round the specie box, but a sequence of ten-inch stud-links, green, encrusted with acorn barnacles, and with a significant crack or two – in short, a derelict cable.

Taking a turn of rope round the cleat, he hauled the links close up to the stern, and freeing them at the cost of a couple of grapnel-teeth, the cable with a sullen *chunk* dropped back to its long repose on the river bed. But valuable time had been lost; he must avoid this spot in the future. Drifting some way off, once more he flung the grapnel overboard, and then resumed his weary cruise.

Time sped, and at least two hours had passed before the boat was brought up with a jerk – the grapnel had caught this time with a vengeance. At first he hauled deliberately, then with all his power, and as the grapnel held he tugged and strained until the sweat rained pit-a-pat from his brow. This, he thought, could be no cable – an anchor perhaps? He took breath, then threw all his weight upon the rope, but not an inch did he gain. He was almost tempted to cut the rope and leave the grappling iron fixed, when all at once he felt it give a little, and slowly came the rope inboard – inch by inch, hand over hand.

Already was he peering for the first glimpse of the chain, when right out from the water grew a thing so startling, so unlooked for, that at the sight the rope slipped through his fingers, and it vanished. But the shock was only momentary. His was a philosophical mind, and before many feet had run overboard he was again hauling lustily.

Again the thing jerked up – to some no doubt a terrifying spectacle; it was a boot, still covering a human foot, and lower down a second showed dimly. Coarse and roughly made, they were the trademarks of a worker, and Pringle asked no sight of the slimy canvas, shredded and rotten, which clung to the limbs below, to be assured that here was the victim of the tragedy whose sole witness he had been. His arms trembled with the immense strain he was putting on them, and, rousing himself, he hauled with might and main to end the task.

Presently, a shapeless, bloated thing floated alongside; and then a box, securely hooked by its crossed-chains, showed clear, the sodden mass floated out to its full length, and as the rope jerked of a sudden it broke loose and floated off upon the tide. Unprepared for so abrupt a lightening of the weight, Pringle slipped and fell in the boat, and the box sank with a noisy rattle of the chain across the gunwale.

In a moment he was on his feet, and, cheered by the prospect of victory, his fatigue vanished. Very soon was the chest at the surface again; then, by a mighty effort and nearly swamping the boat, he dragged it into the stern-sheets. It was a grisly relic he found within the cross-chains. Gripped hard, the arm had dislocated in the awful wrench of the accident; then later, half severed by an agency of which Pringle did not care to think, the work had finally been accomplished by the force which he had just used.

Looking away, he drew his knife, and, hacking the fingers from their death grasp, sent the repulsive object to the depths from which he had raised it. Exhausted and breathless as he was, with characteristic caution, Pringle unshipped the block, and cutting the grapnel-chain from the rope dropped it over the side. He had just stowed the box at his feet, when a sudden concussion nearly flung him to the bottom of the boat.

"Hulloa, there, in the boat!" hailed a peremptory voice. "Why don't you show a light?"

Peeping round the lugsail, Pringle beheld a sight the most unwelcome he could have imagined – a Board of Trade boat, with three men in it, had nearly run him down.

"I've been fishing, and lost my tackle. The night came up before I could beat up against the tide."

"Where have you come from?" inquired the steersman, an officer in charge of the boat.

"From Erith, this afternoon."

"Fishing for tobacco, likely," the other remarked grimly. "Throw us your painter. You must come with us to Gravesend, anyhow."

Pringle went forward and threw them the painter, and stepping back made as if to strike the lugsail, when the officer interposed.

"Hold on there!" he exclaimed. "Keep your sail up – it'll help us against the tide."

Pringle, nothing loth, sat down behind the sail. The officer had not yet seen the box, and for the present the sail helped to conceal it. The address letters and shipping marks were still legible on the case, and any way it was impossible for him to account for its possession legitimately. It was about nine; they would soon be at Gravesend, and once there discovery was inevitable. How on earth was he to escape from this unpleasant situation? Should he sink the box again? But the night was dark, and looking round he could see no friendly buoy or other mark by which to fix the spot in his memory.

Right ahead of them a steamer was coming down with the tide, and the officer edged away towards a large barge at anchor. Nearing her, Pringle noticed she had a dinghy streaming astern, and as they plunged into the deeper gloom she cast he had a sudden inspiration.

Catching the dinghy's painter with his boat-hook, he hauled her alongside, cut the painter, and gradually drawing it in secured it to the cleat in his stern. At once the rowers felt the extra load, and the officer hailed him to trim his sheet. Swiftly making his rope fast to the box-chain, he rove the other end through the ring in the dinghy's bow and knotted it tightly; then, with every muscle taut, scarce daring to breathe in fear of a betraying stertor, he dragged the box over the stern and let the rope run out. With the box depending from her bow, the dinghy sagged along with more than half her keel out of water, and the rowers were audibly cursing the dead weight they had to pull.

"Keep her up there, will you? I'd better come aboard and teach you how to sail!" growled the officer over his shoulder.

Pringle hauled the dinghy close up, cast off her painter, and deftly clambered over the bows, which for an agonizing moment were nearly awash.

"Is that better?" he shouted. And the two boats so quickly shot away from him that he barely caught the cheery answer as, freed from the incubus of dinghy, man, and specie, the escort rowed on to Gravesend.

The tide fast lengthened the space between, and Pringle drifted back until the light of the patrol boat was lost among those ashore; then, with his slight strength, he hauled upon the rope and tumbled the box into the dinghy.

Thud-thud! thud-thud! thud-thud!

A steamer was approaching, and looking round he saw the mast-head lights of a tug with a vessel in tow. Handling the dinghy's sculls, he paddled to one side and waited. On came the tug; at the end of a long warp there followed a three-masted schooner, with an empty boat towing astern of her. As soon as the ship came level with him he pulled diagonally across, and as the boat glided by, seized her with his hand, and for a while the craft ground and rubbed against each other in the swell as he held them side by side.

But the precaution was heedless; the crew of the homeward-bound were too busy looking ahead to notice anything astern.

Going forward and fishing up the painter from the dinghy's bows, he crept back with it, clawing along the boat's gunwale each way, and rove it through the boat's stern-ring. As he made fast, the dinghy swung round to her place in the rear of the procession; and, settling down aft beside the precious box, Pringle was towed upstream.

Gravesend was soon astern, and for the present he felt no fear of the patrol. Whether did they credit him with the feat of swimming off with some contraband object, or with merely falling overboard, they would never have suspected his presence in the dinghy that trailed behind the three-master's boat.

The voyage seemed endless, and as hour lengthened into hour he killed some time by scraping the address and stencil marks from the box. At first he thought they were bound for the Pool; but when the tug began to slow up, about two o'clock, he found they were off the Foreign Cattle Market at Deptford. The tide was now running slack, and, casting off from the boat, he rowed under the stern of a lighter at the end of a double column, all empty, judging by their height above the water; and, throwing his rope round one of the stays of her sternpost, he lay down in the dinghy to rest.

Soon, wearied with his long night's labour and soothed by the ripple of the tide, as turning and running more strongly it eddied round the lighter, he dropped into an uneasy doze. A puffing and slapping noise mingled with his slumbers, and then, as three o'clock struck loudly form the market, he awoke with a start.

At once he had a drowsy sense of movement; but, regarding it as a mere effect of the tide, he tried to settle some plan for the future. Any attempt to go ashore with the box at Deptford he knew would render him suspect of smuggling, and would land him once for all in the hands of the police. Safety, then, lay up the river, and the higher the better. He was thinking of sculling out into the stream and of running up with the tide, even at the risk of being challenged by another patrol, when it suddenly struck him that the shadowy buildings on either bank were receding. He stared harder, and took a bearing between a mast and a chimney stack, and watched them close up and then part again. There was no doubt of it – he was moving! Presently they shot under a wide span, and dimly recognizing the castellated mass of the Tower Bridge he knew that fortune was playing his game for him – or, as he might perhaps have read in manuscript, had his literary agency possessed any reality, "the stars in their courses were fighting for him."

The wind had died away and the night had grown warmer, but although he could have slept fairly in the boat – indeed, would have given worlds to do so – he dared not give way to the temptation. The lighters were bound he knew not whither; he must keep awake to cast off the moment they stopped. To fight his drowsiness he turned to the box again, and spent a little time in furbishing the surface, and finally, detaching the now useless chain, he dropped it overboard.

Gradually, as bridge succeeded bridge, the sky lightened, and as glow behind told the speedy dawn. Up came the sun, while the train of lighters dived beneath a grey stone bridge, and on the left a tall verandahed tower, springing from out a small forest, coruscated in warm red and gold. Pringle started up with a shiver, exclaiming, as the gorgeous sight pictured the idea:

Wake! for the sun, who scattered into flight
  The stars before him from the field of night,
Drives night along with them from heaven, and strikes
  The Sultan's Turret with a shaft of light!

Beside the tower a huge dome blazed like a gigantic arc lamp, and shading his eyes from the glare Pringle made out the familiar lines of the palm house at Kew. This was high enough for his purpose; and while the flotilla, in the wake of a little fussy, bluff-bowed tug, sped onward, he cast off from the barge and sculled leisurely upstream.

The exercise warmed him after his long spell of frigid inaction; he turned towards the Surrey bank, and skirting the grounds of the Observatory ran ashore just beyond the railway bridge. A ragged object, asleep on the towing path, woke up as the boat grounded, and mechanically scratched itself.

"Mind the boat for yer, guv'nor?"

He looked like a tramp. From his obviously impecunious condition he was not likely to be overburdened with scruples.

"Yes; but find me a cab first, and bring it as near as you can."

As the man, scenting a tip, rose with alacrity, Pringle tumbled the box on to the shingle. It now showed little trace of its adventures, was already dry upon the surface, and, clear of the markings, bore an innocent resemblance to a box of ship's cocoa.

It was nearing seven when the emissary returned.

"Keb waitin' for yer up the road by the corner there," he reported.

"Give us a hand with this box, then," said Pringle. "It's quartz, and rather heavy."

"Why, but it's that!" ejaculated the man as he lifted one end with an unwonted expenditure of muscular force.

"Now, look here," said Pringle impressively, as they reached the cab. "I shall be back about noon, and I want you to look after the boat for me till then. That will be five hours – suppose we say at two shillings each?"

The tramp's eyes glistened, and he touched his cap peak.

"Well, here's half a sovereign." Pringle shrewdly discounted the unlikelihood of the man's rendering any part of the service for which he was being paid in advance.

"Right yer are, guv'nor," agreed the tramp cheerfully, and slipped towards the river bank.

The cab, with Pringle and the box inside, had scarcely disappeared round the corner when the tramp made off at a tangent toward Kew, and was seen no more. As to the boat, with a dip and a rock as the tide rose, it floated off into the stream, and resumed its travels in the opposite direction.

The Silver Ingots

The morning was raw, the sun, when it deigned to shine, feeling chill and distant. There was no wind, and as they threaded the curves of the river the occasional funnels wrote persistent sooty lines upon the grey clouds. The park, with its avenues mere damp vistas of naked and grimy boughs, was deserted even by the sparrows, no longer finding a precarious meal at the hands of the children as yet only playing in their slums.

There is little pleasure in cycling towards the end of February, and, preferring walking to the perils of side-slip in the mud, Mr Pringle had walked form Furnival's Inn by way of the Embankment and Grosvenor Road and now sat smoking on the terrace in front of Battersea Park.

There was a new moon, and the rubbish borne during the night on the spring tide from downstream was returning on the ebb to the lower reaches from which it had been ravished. As Mr Pringle smoked and gazed absently at the river, now nearly at its lowest, a large "sou'-wester" caught his eye; it swam gravely with the stream, giving an occasional pirouette as it swirled every now and then into an eddy.

As it floated opposite him he caught a glimpse of some white thing below it – the whole mass seemed to quiver, as if struggling and fighting for life. Could it be a drowning man? Just there the river was solitary; not a soul was visible to help. Vaulting lightly over the low railings, Pringle sprang from the Embankment on to a bed of comparatively clean shingle, which here replaced the odorous mud level, and reached the waterside just as the "sou'-wester", in a more violent gyration, displayed in its grasp a woollen comforter.

Amused and a trifle vexed at his own credulity, Pringle turned, and, walking a yard or two along the beach, tripped and fell as his toe caught in something. Scrambling to his feet, he discovered a loop of half-inch Manila rope, the colour of which told of no long stay there. He gave it a gentle pull, without moving it in the slightest. A harder tug gave no better result; and, his curiosity now thoroughly aroused, he seized it with both hands, and, with his heels dug into the shingle, dragged out of the water just a plaited carpenter's tool-basket.

The rope, in length about six feet, was rove through the handles as if for carrying over the shoulder. Surprised at its weightiness, he peeped inside. They were odd-looking things he found – no mallets or chisels, planes or turnscrews, only half a dozen dirty-looking bricks.

Wondering more and more, he picked one up and examined it carefully. Towards the end was faint suggestion as it were of a scallop-shell, and, turning it over, he detected another and more perfect impression of the same with a crest and monogram, the whole enclosed within an oblong ornamental border, which a closer scrutiny revealed as the handle of a spoon. On another brick he identified a projection as the partially fused end of a candlestick; and, when he scraped off some of the dirt with his knife, the unmistakable lustre of silver met his gaze. All six ingots were of very irregular outline, as if cast in a clumsy or imperfect mould.

A cold sensation about the feet made him look down. Unnoticed by him, the tide had turned and he now stood to the ankles in water. For a moment longer he continued to crouch, while sending a cautious glance about him. In the quarter of an hour or less he had spent by the waterside only a single lighter had passed, and the man in charge had been too much occupied in making the most of the tide to spare any attention ashore. The terrace behind him was quite deserted, and he was sheltered from any observation from the bridge by a projection of the Embankment, which made of the patch of shingle a miniature bay. As to the little steamboat pier, to the naked eye his movements were as indistinguishable from that as from the opposite side of the river. His privacy was complete.

Straightening up, he turned his back on the water and directly faced the terrace. Right in front of him he could see a sycamore standing in the park, and, carefully noting its appearance, he scrambled up the ten feet or so of embankment wall, which at that point was much eroded and gave an easy foothold.

Once on the terrace, he walked briskly up and down to warm his frozen feet, and as he walked he tried to reason out the meaning of his discovery. Here was an innocent-looking carpenter's basket with half a dozen silver ingots of obviously illicit origin – for they had been clumsily made by the fusing together indiscriminately of various articles of plate.

Roughly estimating their weight at about eight pounds apiece, then their aggregate value was something over 100 – not a large sum, perhaps, but no doubt representing the proceeds of more than one burglary. They must have been sunk below low-water mark, say, about a week ago, when they would have been covered at all states of the tide; now, with the onset of the spring tides, they would be exposed twice daily for an hour.

Could the owner have known of this fact? Probably not. Pringle hardly credited him with much skill or premeditation. Such a hiding place rather pointed to a hasty concealment of compromising articles, and the chances were all against the spot having been noted.

On the whole, although it was a comparatively trifling find, Pringle decided it was worth annexing. Nothing could be done for the present, however. By this time the rising tide had concealed even the rope; besides, he could never walk out of the park with a carpenter's basket over his shoulder, even if he were to wait about until it had dried. No; he must return for it in clothing more suited to its possession.

As he walked back to Furnival's Inn, a clock striking half past eleven suggested a new idea. By ten that night the basket would be again exposed, and it might be his last chance of securing it; the morning might see its discovery by someone else. The place was a public one, and although he had been singularly fortunate in its loneliness today, who could tell how many might be there tomorrow? This decided him.

About half past ten that evening Pringle crossed the Albert Bridge to the south side, and turning short off to the left descended a flight of steps which led down to the water; the park gates had been long closed, and this was the only route available. His tall, lithe figure was clothed in a seedy, ill-fitting suit he reserved for such occasions; his tie was of a pattern unspeakable, his face and hands dirty; but although his boots were soiled and unpolished, they showed no further departure from their wonted, and even feminine, neatness. Since the morning his usually fair hair had turned black, and a small strip of whisker had grown upon his clean-shaven face, whilst the port-wine mark emblazoning his right cheek had disappeared altogether.

At the foot of the steps he waited until a nearing wagon had got well upon the bridge, and then, as its thunder drowned his footsteps, he tramped over the shelving beach, and rounding the projection of the embankment found himself in the little bay once more. With his back to the water, he sidled along until opposite the sycamore, and then, facing about, he went down on his hands and knees groping for the loop. Everything seemed as he had left it, and the basket, already loosened from its anchorage, came rattling up the pebbles as soon as he made a very moderate traction on the rope. What with the noise he made himself, slight though it was, and his absorption in the work, Pringle never heard a gentle step approaching by the path he had himself taken; but as he hastily arranged the ingots on the beach, and was about to hold the basket up to drain, his arm was gripped by a muscular hand.

"Fishing this time of night?" inquired a refined voice in singular contrast to the rough appearance of the speaker. Then, more sharply, "Come – get up! Let's have a look at you."

Pringle rose in obedience to the upward lift upon his arm, and as the two men faced each other the stranger started, exclaiming:

"So it's you, is it! I thought we should meet again some day."

"Meet again?" repeated Pringle stupidly, as for about the second or third time in his life his presence of mind deserted him.

"Don't say you've forgotten me at Wurzleford last summer! Let's see – what was your name? I ought to remember it, too – ah, yes, Courtley! Have you left the Church, Mr Courtley? Seem rather down on your luck now. Why, Solomon in all his glory wasn't in it with you at Wurzleford? And you don't seem to need your glasses, either. Has your sight improved?"

Pringle remembered him before he had got halfway through his string of sarcasms. He had not altered in the least, the shell might be rough, but the voice and manner of the gentleman burglar were as Chesterfieldian as ever. Of all people in the world, he was the one whom Pringle would have least desired to see at that moment and he prepared himself for a very bad quarter of an hour.

"It's lucky for you we haven't met before," continued the other. "If I could have got at you that night, it would have been your life or mine! Don't think I've forgiven you. I must say, though, you did it very neatly; it's something, I can tell you, to get the better of me. Why, I've never dared to breathe a word of it since; I should be a laughing stock for the rest of my days. I, the 'Toff', as they call me!

"But I can see a joke, even if it's against myself, and I've laughed several times since when I've thought of it. Fancy locking me in that room while you coolly walked off with the stuff that I'd been working for for months. And such stuff too! I think you'd have done better to act squarely with me. Those rubies don't seem to have done you much good. I never thought you'd do much with them at the time. It needs a man with capital to plant such stuff as that. But what's the game now? Who put you up to this?"

He had been taking short steps up and down the beach, half soliloquizing as he walked, and now he broke off abruptly and fronted Pringle.

"No one." Pringle had now recovered his self-possession. They were alone; it was man to man, and anyhow, the "Toff" did not seem to be very vindictive.

"Then how did you know it was here? You're a smart fellow, I know; but I don't think you're quite smart enough to see to the bottom of the river."

"It was quite accidental," said Pringle frankly. "It was this way." And he sketched the doings of the morning.

"Upon my word," exclaimed the "Toff", "you and I seem fated to cross one another's paths. But I'll be kinder than you deserve. This stuff" – he kicked the ingots – "is the result of a 'wedge-hunt', as we call it. Nervous chap, bringing it up the river, got an idea that he was being shadowed – dropped it from a steamer three days ago – wasn't certain of his bearings when he had done it. That comes of losing one's head. Now, if it hadn't been for you, I might never have found it, although it looks as if I was right in calculating the tides and so on. As you seem in rather hard case, I'll see you're not a loser over the night's work so long as you make yourself useful."

Pringle assented cheerfully; he was curious to see the end of it all. While the other was speaking he had decided to fall in with his humour. Indeed, unless he fled in cowardly retreat, there was nothing else to be done. The "Toff", as he knew, was wiry, but although in good form himself, Pringle's arm throbbed and tingled where it had been gripped. They were equally matched so far as strength went, unless the "Toff" still carried a revolver. Besides, the ingots were not worth disputing over. Had they been gold now – !

"Well, just lend a hand then." And, the "Toff" producing some cotton-waste, they commenced to pack the ingots back into the basket.

"Look here," the "Toff" continued as they worked; "why don't you join me? You want someone to advise you, I should say. Whatever your game was at Wurzleford, you don't seem to have made much at it, nor out of me, either – ah!"

The subject was evidently a sore one, and the "Toff's" face hardened and he clenched his hands at the memories it aroused.

"Yes," he went on, "you seem a man of some resource, and if only you'd join me, what with that and my experience – why, we'd make our pile and retire in a couple of years! And what a life it is! Talk of adventure and excitement and all that – what is there to equal it? Canting idiots talk of staking one's liberty. Liberty, indeed! Why, what higher stake can one play for? – except one's life, and I've done that before now. I've played for a whole week at Monte Carlo, and believe I broke the bank (I couldn't tell for certain – they don't let you know, and never close till eleven, in spite of all people think and talk to the contrary); I've played poker with some of the cutest American players; I've gambled on the Turf; I've gambled on the Stock Exchange; I've run Kanakas to Queensland; I've smuggled diamonds; I've hunted big game all over the world; I've helped to get a revolution in Ecuador, and nearly (ha! ha!) got myself made President; I've – hang it, what haven't I done?

"And I tell you there's nothing in all I've gone through to equal the excitement of the life I'm leading now. Then, too, we're educated men. I'm Rugby and John's, and that's where I score over most I have to work with; they sicken me with their dirty, boozy lives. They have a bit of luck, then they're drunk for a month, and have to start again without a penny, and the rats running all over them. Now, we two – Gentle! Don't take it by the handles. Wait a second. D'you hear anything?"

A cab trotted over the wooden-paved bridge, then silenced again. The "Toff" wound one end of the rope round and round his wrist, and motioned Pringle to do the same; then, with a sign to tread warily, he started to make the circuit of the promontory, the basket swaying between them as they kept step. Pringle, with an amused sense of the other's patronizing airs, followed submissively behind him up the shelving beach. By the wooden steps the "Toff" paused.

"Under here," he directed; and they stuffed the basket under the bottom step.

"Now," he murmured in Pringle's ear, "you go up to the road, and if you see no one about walk a little way down, as if you'd come off the bridge, and stamp your feet like this." He stamped once or twice, as if to restore the circulation in his feet, but with a rhythmical cadence in the movement.

"Yes; what then?"

"There ought to be a trap waiting down the first turning on the opposite side of the road. If it doesn't come up, count twenty and stamp again."

"And then?"

"If nothing happens, come back and tell me."

When he stood at the top of the stairs Pringle felt much inclined, instead of turning to the left, to go the other way and cross the bridge, leaving the "Toff" to secure the ingots as best he could. Later on he had cause to regret that he had not done so; but for the moment love of adventure prevailed and, walking down the gradient form the bridge, he gave the signal. There was no one in sight, but the action was such a natural one on a damp and foggy night that had the street been ever so crowded it would have passed unnoticed.

Pringle counted twenty, and repeated the signal. By this time he had reached the corner, and looking down the side street, he distinctly saw the twin lights of a carriage advancing at a trot. He turned back and reached the stairs as a rubber-tyred miniature brougham pulled up beside him.

"Is it there?" whispered the "Toff" impatiently.

"There's a brougham stopping. I don't know – "

"Yes, yes; that's it. Lend a hand, now; we mustn't keep it waiting about."

Marvelling at the style in which the "Toff" appeared to work, Pringle helped to lug the basket up, and between them they bundled it into the carriage.

"Now," said the "Toff", fumbling in his waistcoat pocket, "what do you say about my proposal?"

"Well, really, I should like to think over it a little," replied Pringle evasively.

"Oh, I can't wait here all night while you're making up your mind. If you don't recognize a good thing when you see it, you're not the man for me. It's not everyone I should make the offer to."

"Then I think I had better say 'No'."

"Please yourself, and sink a little lower than you are." The "Toff" appeared nettled at Pringle's refusal. He ceased to grope in his waistcoat, and drawing a leather purse from his trouser pocket took something from it. "That's for your trouble," said he shortly; and the next minute was bowling swiftly over the bridge.

Pringel, who had mechanically extended his hand, found by the glimmer of a lamp that the "Toff" had appraised his services at the sum of seven shillings, and was moved to throw the coins into the river. As he hesitated over the fate of the florin and two half-crowns in his palm, a policeman approached and glanced suspiciously at him. His hand closed on the money, and he passed on to the bridge. He felt hot and grimy with his exertions; also his boots were damp, and the night wind began to grow chilly. Halfway across he broke into a run, the elastic structure swaying perceptibly beneath his feet. Over the other side the lights of a public house pierced the mist, and he struck into the roadway towards it.

"Outside – on the right!" said a voice, as he opened the door of the saloon bar. For the time he had forgotten the shabbiness of his dress, enhanced as it was by the many things it had suffered in the course of the night's work, and with an unwonted diffidence he sought the public bar. There, with a steaming glass in hand, he strove to dry his boots at a gas stove in one corner, but he still felt cold and miserable when, about half past eleven, he rose to go.

"Ere – what's this?" The barman had inserted the proffered coin in a *trier*, and giving it a deft jerk, now flung it, bent nearly double, across the counter.

"I beg your pardon," Pringle apologized, as he produced another. "I had no idea it was bad."

The barman threw the second coin upon the counter. It rang clearly, but doubled in the *trier* like so much putty.

"Bad!" chorused the onlookers.

"Fetch a constable, Ted!" was the solo of the landlord, who had come round from the other side of the bar.

For the second time that evening Pringle's nerve took flight. A horrible idea seized him – a crevasse seemed to open at his feet. Had the "Toff" played some treachery upon him? And as the door swung after the potman, he made a break for liberty. But the barman was quick as he, and with a cat-like spring over the counter, he held Pringle before he had got half across the threshold, several customers officiously aiding.

"I'm going to prosecute this man," announced the landlord; adding, for the benefit of the audience generally, "I've taken six bad half-crowns this week."

"Swine! Serve 'im right! Oughter be shot!" were the virtuous comments on this statement.

As resistance was clearly useless Pringle submitted to his arrest, and was presently accompanied to the police station by an escort of most of the loafers in the bar.

"What's your name?" asked the night inspector, as he took the charge.

Pringle hesitated. He realized that appearances were hopelessly against him. Attired as he was, to give his real name and address would only serve to increase suspicion, while a domiciliary visit to Furnival's Inn on the part of the police was to be avoided at all costs; the fiction of his literary agency as spurious as the coins which had landed him in his present plight, would be the very least discovery to reward them.

"Now, then, what is it?" demanded the inspector impatiently.

"Augustus Stammers," Pringle blurted, on the spur of the moment.

"Ah! I thought you were a stammerer," was the facetious remark of the publican.

The inspector frowned his disapproval. "Address?" he queried. Pringle again hesitated. "No fixed?" the inspector suggested.

"No fixed," agreed Pringle; and having replied to subsequent inquiries that his age was forty and his occupation a carpenter, he was ordered to turn out his pockets. Obediently he emptied his belongings on the desk, and as his money was displayed the landlord uttered a triumphant shout.

"There y'are!" he exclaimed, pouncing on a bright half-crown. "That makes three of 'em!"

This incriminatory evidence, together with a knife, being appropriated, Pringle was led away down some steps, through a courtyard, and then into a long whitewashed passage flanked by doors on either side. Pushing one open, "In you go," said his conductor; and Pringle having walked in the door was shut and locked behind him.

Though lighted by a gas jet in the passage which shone through a small window above the door, the cell was rather dim, and it was some little while before his eyes, accustomed to the gloom, could properly take in his surroundings. It was a box of a place, about fourteen feet by six, with a kind of wooden bench fixed across the far end, and on this he sat down and somewhat despondently began to think.

It was impossible for Pringle to doubt that he was the victim of the "Toff's" machinations. He remembered how the latter's manner had changed when he positively refused the offer of partnership; how the "Toff" had ceased searching in his vest, and had drawn the purse from his trouser pocket. He supposed at the time that the "Toff", nettled at his refusal, had substituted silver for gold, and had thought it strange that he should keep his gold loose and his silver in a purse. It all stood out clear and lucid enough now. "Snide" money, as he knew, must always be treated with gentleness and care, and, lest it should lose the bloom of youth, some artists in the line are even accustomed to wrap each piece separately in tissue paper. The "Toff" evidently kept his "snide" in a purse, and, feeling piqued, had seized the opportunity of vindictively settling a score.

Pringle cursed his folly in not having foreseen such a possibility. What malicious fate was it that curbed his first impulse to sink the "Toff's" generosity in the river? With all his experience of the envious ways of his fellow men, after all his fishing in troubled waters, to be tricked like this – to be caught like vermin in a trap! Well might the "Toff" sneer at him as an amateur! And most galling of all was the reflection that he was absolutely guiltless of any criminal intent. But it was useless to protest his innocence; a long term of imprisonment was the least he could expect. It was certainly the tightest place in which he had ever found himself.

Pringle was, fortunately, in no mood for sleep. He had soon received unmistakable evidence of the presence of the third of Pharaoh's plagues, and sought safety in constant motion. Besides, there were other obstacles to repose. From down the passage echoed the screams and occasional song of a drunken woman, as hysteria alternated with pleasurable ideas in her alcoholic brain; nearer, two men, who were apparently charged together, kept up an interchange of abuse from distant cells, each blaming the other for the miscarriage of their affairs; right opposite, the thunderous snoring of a drunken man filled the gaps when either the woman slumbered or the rhetoric of the disputants failed. Lastly, at regular intervals, a constable opened a trap in the cell doors to ascertain by personal observation and inquiry the continued existence of the inmates.

As time passed the cells overflowed, and every few minutes Pringle heard the tramp of feet and the renewed unlocking and sorting out as fresh guests were admitted to the hospitality of the State.

After a time the cell opposite was opened, and the voice of the snorer arose. He objected to a companion, as it seemed, and threatened unimaginable things were one forced upon him. He was too drunk to be reasoned with, so a moment after Pringle's door was flung open, and at the decision, "This un'll do," his solitude was at an end.

It was a dishevelled, dirty creature who entered; also his clothes were torn rawly as from a recent struggle. He slouched in with his hands in his pockets, and with a side glance at Pringle, flung himself down on the bench. Presently he expectorated as a preliminary to conversation, and with a jerk of the head towards the opposite cell, "I'd rawther doss wiv' im than wiv' a wet unbreller! What yer in for, guv'nor?"

"I'm charged with passing bad money," replied Pringle affably.

"Anyone wiv' yer?"

"No."

"Ow many'd yer got on yer?"

"They found three."

A long whistle.

"That's all three stretch for yer! Why didn't yer work the pitch 'long o' someone else? Yer ought ter 'ave 'ad a pal outside to 'old the snide, while you goes in wiv' only one on yer, see?"

Pringle humbly acknowledged the error, and his companion, taking pity on his greenness in the lower walks of criminality, then proceeded to give him several hints, the following of which, he assured Pringle, would be "slap-up claws"!

Later on he grew confidential, told how his present "pinching" was due to "collerin' a red jerry from a ole reeler," and presently, pleading fatigue, he laid him down on the bench and was soon snoring enviably. But his slumbers were fitful, for, although but little inconvenienced by the smaller inhabitants of the cell, having acquired a habit of allowing for them without waking, he was periodically roused by the gaoler's inspection. On many of these occasions he would sit up and regale Pringle for a time with such further scraps of autobiography as he appeared to pride himself on – always expecting his present misfortune, which, after his preliminary burst of confidence, he seemed anxious to ignore as a discreditable incident, being "pinched over a reeler". In this entertaining manner they passed the night until eight o'clock, when Pringle authorized the expenditure of some of his capital on a breakfast of eggs and bacon and muddy coffee from "outside", his less affluent companion having to content himself with the bare official meal.

Soon after breakfast a voice form a near cell rose in earnest colloquy. "Hasn't my bail come yet, gaoler?"

"I tell yer 'e's wired 'e'll come soon's 'e's 'ad 'is breakfast."

"But I've got a most important engagement at nine! Can't you let me out before he comes?"

"Don't talk tommy-rot! You've got to go up to the court at ten. If yer bail comes, out yer'll go; if it doesn't, yer'll have to go on to Westminster."

"Must I go in the van? Can't I have a cab – I'm only charged with being excited!"

"Yer'll 'ave to go just like everybody else."

Bang! went the trap in the door, and as the footsteps died up the passage Pringle's companions chanted:

But the pore chap doesn't know, yer know –
'E 'asn't bin in London long!

About an hour later the cells were emptied, and the prisoners were marched down to the courtyard and packed away in the police van to be driven the short intervening distance to Westminster Police Court. There was no lack of company here. On arrival the van-riders were turned into a basement room, already half full, and well lighted by an amply barred window which, frosted as were its panes, allowed the sun freely to penetrate as if to brighten the over-gloomy thoughts of those within.

Punctually at ten the name of the first prisoner was called. It was the hysterical lady of the police cells, who disappeared amid loudly expressed wishes of "Good luck!" The wait was a tedious one, and as the crowd dwindled, Pringle's habitual stoicism enabled him to draw a farcical parallel between his fellows and a dungeonful of aristocrats awaiting the tumbril during the Reign of Terror. The noisy converse around him consisted chiefly of speculations as to the chances of each one being either remanded, "fullied", or summarily convicted.

Pringle had no inclination to join therein; besides, his overnight companion had long ago decided, with judicial precision, that he would be either "fullied" – that is, fully committed for trial – or else remanded for inquiries, but that the chances were in favour of the latter.

The room was half empty when Pringle's summons came, but the call for "Stammers" at first brought no response. He had quite forgotten his alias (not at all an unusual thing, by the way, with those who acquire such a luxury), and it was not until the gaoler repeated the name and everyone looked questioningly at his neighbour that Pringle remembered his ownership and passed out, acknowledging with a wave of the hand the chorus of "Good-luck" prescribed by the etiquette of the place.

Up a flight of steps, and along a narrow passage to a door, where he was halted for a season. A subdued hum of voices could be heard within. Suddenly the door opened.

"Three months, blimey, the 'ole image! Jus' cos my 'usband 'it me!"

And as a red-faced matron, with a bandaged head, flounced past him on her way downstairs, Pringle stepped into the iron-railed pen she had just vacated. In front of him was a space of some yards occupied by three or four desked seats, and on the bench beyond sat a benevolent-looking old gentleman with a bald head, whom Pringle greeted with a respectful bow.

The barman was at once called; he had little to say, and said it promptly.

"Any questions?" Pringle declined the clerk's invitation, and the police evidence, officially concise, followed.

"Any questions?" No, again.

"Is anything known of him?" inquired the old gentleman.

An inspector rose from the well in front of the bench, and said:

"There have been a number of cases in the neighbourhood lately, sir, and I sould be glad of a remand to see if he can be identified."

"Very well. Remanded for a week." And so, after a breathless hearing of about two and three-quarter minutes by the clock, Pringle found himself standing outside the court again.

" 'Ow long 'ave yer got?" Instead of going along the passage, Pringle had been turned into a room which stood handy at the foot of the steps, where he was greeted by a number of (by this time) old acquaintances.

"I'm remanded for a week."

"Same 'ere," observed his cell-fellow of the night before. "I'll see yer, mos' likely, at the show."

"Any bloke for the 'Ville?" inquired a large, red-faced gentleman, with a pimple of a nose which he accentuated by shaving clean.

"Yus; I've got six months," said one.

"Garn!" contemptuously replied the face. "Yer'll go to the Scrubbs."

"Garn yerself!" retorted the other; and as the discussion at once became warm and general Pringle sat down in a far corner, where the disjointed shreds of talk fused into an odd patchwork.

" 'E sayd you're charged with a vurry terrible thing, sayd 'e (hor! hor! hor!). I tell yer, ef yer wants the strite tip – don't you flurry yer fat, now – so, says I, then yer can swear to my character – they used to call it cocoa-castle, strite they did – "

"Answer your names, now!" The gaoler was holding the door open. Beside him stood a sergeant with a sheaf of blue papers, from which he called the names, and as each man answered he was arranged in order along the passage. It was a welcome relief. Pringle began to feel faint, having eaten nothing since the morning, and, what with the coarse hilarity and the stuffy atmosphere by which he had been environed so many hours, his head ached distractingly.

"Forward now – keep your places!" The procession tramped into an open yard, where a police van stood waiting. With much clattering of bars, jingling of keys, and banging of doors, the men, to the number of a dozen or so, were packed into the little sentry boxes which ran round the inside of the van, its complement being furnished by four or five ladies, brought from another part of the establishment. This done, the sergeant, closing the door after him, gave the word to start, and the heavy van, lumbering out of the yard, rolled down the street like a ship in a gale.

"Gimme a light," said a voice close to the little trap in Pringle's cell door. Looking out, he found he was addressed by a youth in the opposite box, who extended a cigarette across the corridor.

"Sorry, I haven't got one," Pringle apologized.

" 'Ere y'are," came from the box on Pringle's right, and a smouldering stump was handed to the youth, who proceeded to light another from it.

"'Ave a whiff, guv'nor?" courteously offered the invisible owner. An obscene paw, holding the returned fag, appeared at the aperture.

"No, thanks," declined Pringle hastily.

"Las' chance for a week," urged the man, with genuine altruism.

"I don't smoke," protested Pringle to spare his feelings, adding, as the van turned off the road and came to a stand, "Is this the House of Detention?"

"No; this is the 'Ville."

The van rumbled under an archway, and then, after more banging, jingling, and clattering, half a dozen men were extracted from the boxes and deposited in the yard.

"Goodbye, Bill! Keep up yer sperrits!" screamed a soprano from the inmost recesses of the van.

"Come and meet us at the fortnight," growled a deepest base from the courtyard.

A calling of names, the tramp of feet, then silence for a while, only broken by the champing of harness. Presently a brisk order, and, rumbling through the arch again, they were surrounded by the noise of traffic. But it was not for long; a few minutes, seconds even, and they halted once more, while heavy doors groaned apart. Then, clattering through a portico full of echoes, and describing a giddy curve, the van abruptly stopped as an iron gate crashed dismally in the rear.

" 'Ere we are guv'nor!" remarked the altruist.

The House of Detention

Clang, clang! Clang-a-clang, clang!

As the bell continued to ring Mr Pringle started from an unrestful slumber, and, sitting up in bed, stared all around. Everything was so painfully white that his eyes closed spasmodically.

White walls, white-vaulted ceiling, even the floor was whitish-coloured – all white, but for the black door-patch at one end, and on this he gazed for respite from the glare. Slowly he took it all in – the bare table-slab, the shelf with its little stack of black volumes, the door, handleless and iron-sheeted, above all the twenty-four little squares of ground glass with their horizontal bars broadly shadowed in the light of the winter morning.

It was no dream, then, he told himself.

The thin mattress, only a degree less harsh than the plank bed beneath, was too insistent, obstinately as he might close his eyes to all beside. And, as he sat, the events of the last six and thirty hours came crowding through his memory. How clearly he saw it all! Not a detail was missing.

Again he stood by the riverside, the bare trees dripping in the mist; again he saw the ingots, and lent unwilling aid to save them, fingered the contemptuous vails, sole profit of their discovery. He was crossing the bridge; beyond shone the lights of the tavern, and there within he saw the frowsy crowd of loafers, and the barman proving the base coin he innocently tendered. And then came the arrest, the police cell, the filthy sights and sounds, the court with its sodden, sickening atmosphere, and, last of all, the prison, What a trap had he, open-eyed, walked into! For a second he ground his teeth in impotent fury.

The bell ceased. Dejectedly he rose, wondering as to the toilet routine of the establishment. Shaving was not to be thought of, he supposed, but enforced cleanliness was a thing he had read of somewhere. How long would last night's bath stand good for? He looked at the single coarse brown towel and shuddered. Footsteps approached; he heard voices and the jingling of keys, then the lock shot noisily, and the door was flung open.

"Now, then, put out your slops and roll your bedding up."

Pringle obeyed, but his bed-making was so lavish of space that when the warder peeped in again, some ten minutes later, he regarded the heap with a condescending grin, and presently returned with a prisoner who deftly rolled the sheets and blankets into a bundle whose end-on view resembled a variegated archery target. Then the hinges creaked once more, the lock snapped, and Pringle was left to his meditations. They were not of a cheerful nature, and it was with an exceeding bitter smile that he set himself to seriously review his position. Already had he decided that to reveal himself as the proprietor of that visionary literary agency in Furnival's Inn would only serve to increase the suspicion that already surrounded him, while availing nothing to free him from the present charge – even if it did not result in fresh accusations! On the other hand, unless he did so he could see no way of obtaining any money from his bankers so to avail himself of the very small loophole of escape which a legal defence might afford.

He had one consolation – a very small one, it is true. Money is never without its uses, and it was with an eye to future contingencies that he had managed to secrete a single half-sovereign on first arriving at the gaol. Whilst waiting, half-undressed, to enter the searching room, he bethought him of a strip of old-fashioned court plaster which he was accustomed to carry in his pocketbook. He took it out, and, waiting his opportunity, stuck half a sovereign upon it and then pressed the strip against his shin, where it held fast.

"What's that?" inquired a warder a few minutes later, as Pringle stood stripped beneath a measuring gauge.

"I grazed my skin a couple of days ago," said he glibly.

"Graze on right shin!" repeated the warder mechanically to a colleague who was booking Pringle's description; and that was how the coin escaped discovery such time as he was being measured, weighed, searched, examined, and made free of the House of Detention. As he paced up and down the cell, occasionally fingering the little disc in his pocket, its touch did something to leaven his first sensations of helplessness, but they returned with pitiless logic so soon as he thought of escape. Bribery with such a sum was absurd, and he saw only too plainly that the days of Trenck and Casanova were gone for ever.

Chafing at the thought of his sorry fate, Pringle turned for distraction to the inscription which on all sides adorned the plaster walls. They were scarcely so ornate as those existing in the Tower, and their literary merit was of the scantiest; nevertheless they were not without human interest, especially to a fellow sufferer like Pringle.

The first he lighted on appeared to be the record of a deserter: "Alf. Toppy out of Scrubbs 2nd May, now pulled for deserting from 2nd Batt. W Norfolk."

"H Allport" informed all whom it might concern that he was "pinched for felony". Another soldier — it is to be hoped not a criminal — was indicated by the simple record, "Johore, Chitral, Rawal Pindi." One prisoner had summed up his self-compassion in the ejaculation, "Poor old Dick!"

"Cheer up, mate, you'll be out some day," was no doubt intended to be comforting, whilst there was a suggestion of tragedy in the statement, "I am an innocent man charged with felony by an intoxicated woman."

It seemed to be the felonious etiquette for the prisoners to give their addresses as well as their names – thus, "Dave Conolly from Mint Street."

"Dick Callaghan, Lombard Street, Boro, anyone going that way tell Polly Regan I expect nine moon," set Pringle wondering why on earth Dick had not written to Polly and delivered his message for himself. An ingenuous youth was "Willie, from Dials, fullied for taking a kettle without asking for it," with his artless postscript, "only wanted to know the time," but perhaps he passed for a humorist among his acquaintances, while "Darky, from Sailor's kip the Highway, nicked for highway robbery with violence," had a matter-of-fact ruffianism about it which spoke for itself.

From these sordid archives Pringle turned to the printed rules hanging from a peg in the cell, but they were couched in such an aridly official style as to remind him but the more cruelly of his position, and in considerable depression he resumed his now familiar tour – four paces to the window, a turn, and four paces back again, which was the utmost measure of the floor space.

He had almost ceased to regard any plan of escape as feasible, when the idea of Freemasonry occurred as a last resort. Amongst his other studies of human nature Pringle had not neglected the mummeries of The Craft; he had even attained the eminence of a "Grand Zerubbabel". Now, he thought, was the time to test the efficacy of the doctrines he had absorbed and expounded; he would try the effect of masonic symbolism upon the warder.

Soon again the keys rattled and the doors banged; nearer came the sounds, the echoes louder, but now there was a clattering as of tinware. The door was flung open, the warder took a small cube loaf of brown bread from the tray carried by a prisoner, and slapped it, with a tin resembling a squat beer can, down on the table board. The tin was full of hot cocoa, and, quickly raising it with a peculiar motion of the hand, Pringle inquired genially, "How old is your mother?"

The warder stopped in the act of shutting the door; he pulled it open again, and glared speechless at the audacious questioner.

For quite a minute he stood; then, with an accent which his emotion only rendered the purer, he growled:

"None of yer larrks now, me man!"

As the door slammed Pringle mechanically tore the coarse brown bread into fragments, and soaking them in the cocoa swallowed them unheedingly. His last scheme had gone the same road as its predecessors, and he no longer attempted to blind himself to the consequences. He scarcely noticed when the breakfast ware was collected, silently handing out his tins in obedience to the summons.

He was still sitting on the stool, with eyes staring at the frosted windows which his thoughts saw far through and beyond, when the eternal unlocking began again. Listlessly he heard a voice repeating something at every door; he did not catch the words, but there was a tramp of many feet, and a bell was ringing. The voice grew louder; now it was at the next cell. He stood up.

"Chapel!"

Pringle stared at the warder – a fresh one this time.

"Get yer prayer book and 'ymm book, and come to chapel! Put yer badge on," he added, looking back for a minute before continuing his monotonous chant.

Pringle picked up the black volumes and sent an inquiring glance around for the "badge". Prisoner after prisoner defiled past the open door as he waited; then all at once he saw the warder's meaning. Each man displayed a yellow badge upon his breast, and, looking round again, he saw, dangling upon his own gas burner, a similar disc of felt, with the number of the cell stamped upon it. Hanging the tab upon his coat button, Pringle entered a gap in the procession duly labelled "B.3.6." for the occasion.

Right overhead an endless column marched; on the gallery below he saw another, and all around was a rhythmic tramp-tramp in one and the same direction. Down a slope of stairs they went, across a flying bridge, and then along a gallery whose occupants had preceded them. Tramp, tramp; tramp, tramp. Another bridge, and then a door opened into a huge barn of a hall.

Backless forms were ranged in long rows over the wooden floor, with here and there a little pew-like desk, from which the warders piloted their charges to their seats. The prisoner ahead of him was the end man of his bench, and Pringle, motioned to the next one, headed the file along it and sat down by the wall at the far end, with a warder in one of the little pews just in front.

"What yer in for, guv'nor?" asked someone in a husky growl.

Pringle looked round, but his immediate neighbour was glaring stolidly at the nearest warder, whose eye was upon them, and there was no one else within speaking distance but a decrepit old creature, obviously very deaf, on the row behind, and beyond him again a man of apparent education wearing a frock coat. From neither of these could such an inquiry have proceeded.

"Eyes front there! Don't let me catch you looking round again." It was the warder who spoke in peremptory tones, and Pringle started at the words like a corrected schoolboy.

"Hymn number three."

The chaplain had taken his stand by the altar, and the opening bars of Bishop Ken's grand old hymn sounded from the organ. There was a rustle and shuffling of many feet as the whole assembly rose, the organist started the singing, and the many-voiced followed on with a roar which could not wholly slaughter the melody. Halfway through the first verse Pringle felt a nudge in the ribs, and, barely inclining his head, caught the eye of his stolid neighbour as it closed in a grotesque wink. Keeping one eye on the little pew in front the man edged towards him, and repeated, in a sing-song which fairly imitated the air of the hymn:

"What yer in for, matey?"

Taking his cue, Pringle changed back:

"Snide coin," and then a strange duet was sung to the old Genevan air.

"Fust time?"

"Yes."

"Do a bloke a turn?"

"What's that?"

"Change badges – I'll tell yer why at exercise presently. Won't 'urt you, an' do me a sight er good!"

The hymn ceased, and the chaplain began to intone the morning prayers. As they all sat down, Pringle's neighbour dropped his badge on the floor, and, pretending to reach for it, motioned to him to exchange.

The warder's attention was elsewhere, and Pringle obligingly re-labelled himself "C.2.24."

A short and somewhat irrelevant address, another hymn, and the twenty minutes' service was over. As bench after bench emptied, the monotonous tramp again echoed through the bare chamber, and a dusty haze rose and obscured the texts upon the altar. It was a single long procession that snaked round and round the corridors, and, descending by a fresh series of stairways and bridges, disappeared far below in the basement. The lower they got, the atmosphere became sensibly purer, and less redolent of humanity, until at the very bottom Pringle felt a rush of air, welcome for all its coldness, and there, beyond an open grille, was an expanse of green bordered by shrubs, and, above all, the cheery sunlight.

"And earth laughed back at the day," he murmured.

The grass was cut up by concentric rings of flagstones, and round these the prisoners marched at a brisk rate. Between every two rings were stone pedestals, each adorned with a warder, who from this elevation endeavoured to preserve a regulation space between the prisoners – that is to say, when he was not engaged in breathing almost equally futile threatenings against the conversation which hummed from every man who was not immediately in front of him. And what a jumble of costumes! Tall hats mingled with bowlers and seedy caps that surely no man would pick from off a rubbish heap. Here the wearer of a frock-suit followed one who was literally a walking rag shop; and, conspicuous among all with its ever-rakish air in the sober daytime, an opera hat spoke of hilariously twined vine leaves.

"Thankee, guv'nor," came a hoarse whisper from behind Pringle; "yer done me a good turn, yer 'ave so!"

The speaker was slight and sinuously active, with a cat-like gait – a typical burglar; also his hair was closely cropped in the style of the New Cut, which is characterized by a brow-fringe analogous to a Red Indian's scalp-lock, being chivalrously provided for your opponent to clutch in single combat.

"What do you want my badge for?" inquired Pringle with less artistic gruffness.

"Why, the splits'll be 'ere in a minute ter look at us – bust 'em! An' I'll be spotted – what ho! Well, they'll take my number from this badge o' yourn, 'B.3.6.' an' they'll look up your name an' think it's a alias of mine – see? An' then they'll go an' enter all my convictions 'gainst you – haw, haw!"

"Against me! But, I say, you know – "

"Don't you fret – it'll do you no 'arm! Now when I goes up on remand termorrer there won't be nothing returned 'gainst me, so the beak'll let me off light 'stead o' bullyin' me – "

"Yes, yes; I see where you come in right enough," interrupted Pringle. "But what about me?"

"No fear, I tells yer strite. When yer goes up again, if the split ain't found out 'is mistake an' goes ter say anythink 'gainst yer respectability, jest you sing out loud an' say it's all a bit o' bogie – see? Then the split'll see it's not me, an' 'e'll 'ave ter own up, an' p'raps the beak'll be that concerned for yer character bein' took away that he'll – "

"Halt!"

Pringle, in amused wonderment at the cleverness of an idea founded, like all true efforts of genius, on very simple premises, walked into the man ahead of him, who had stopped at the word of command. Those in the inner circle were being moved into the outermost one, and there the whole gathering was packed close and faced inwards.

Measured footsteps were now audible; but when the leaders of this new contingent came in view it was clear that whatever else they might be they were certainly not a fresh batch of prisoners. For one thing, they wore no badges; moreover, they conversed freely as they drew near. Well set up, and with a carriage only to be acquired by drilling, they displayed a trademark in their boots of a uniform type of stoutness.

"Tecs, the swabs!" was the quite superfluous remark of Pringle's neighbour. Along the line they passed, scanning each man's features, now exchanging a whispered comment, and anon making an entry in their pocketbooks. Pringle himself was passed by indifferently, but it was quite otherwise with the wearer of badge "B.3.6." He, evidently a born actor, underwent the scrutiny with an air of profound indifference, which he managed to sustain even when one of the police returned for a second look at his familiar features.

"Forward!"

As the recognizers left the yard the prisoners were sorted out again, and resumed their march round the paved circles.

"That's a bit of all right, guv'ner!" And Pringle's new friend chuckled as he spoke. "Haw, haw! See that split come ter 'ave another look at me? Strite, I nearly busted myself tryin' not ter laugh right out! Shouldn't I like ter see the bloke's face when yer goes up — oh, daisies! Yer never bin copped afore?"

"No. Is there any chance of getting out?"

"What — doin' a bolt? Bless yer innercent young 'art, not from a stir like this! Yer might get up a mutiny, p'raps," he reflected, "so's yer could knock the screws (warders) out. But 'ow are yer ter do that when yer never gets a chance ter 'ave a jaw with more than one at a time? There's the farm now," indicating an adjacent building with a jerk of the head.

"The what?"

"Orspital. If yer feel down on yer luck yer might try ter fetch it, p'raps. But it's no catch 'ere where yer've no work and grups yerself if yer like. Now, when yer've got a stretch the farms clahssy."

Again the bell rang, and the spaces grew wider as the prisoners were marched off by degrees. On the stairs, as they went in, Pringle

95

and his new friend exchanged badges, and the old prisoner, with a muttered "Good luck", passed to his own side of the gaol and was seen no more.

Back in the solitude of his cell Pringle found plentiful matter for thought. The events of the morning had enlarged his mental horizon, and roused fresh hopes of escaping the fate that menaced him. As his long legs measured the cell – one, two, three, four, round again at the door – so lightened was his heart that he once caught himself in the act of whistling softly, while the hours flew by unnoticed.

He swallowed his dinner almost without tasting it, and the clatter of supper tins was all that reminded him that he had eaten nothing for five hours. He was not conscious of much appetite; after all, haricot beans are filling, and a meal more substantial than the pint of tea and brown loaf might have been thrown away upon him. With supper the gas had been kindled, and as he sat and munched his bread at the little table, the badge suspended on the bracket shown golden in the light.

Since morning he had endowed it with a special interest – indeed, it largely inspired the thoughts which now cheered him. True, it was not a talisman at whose approach the prison doors would open wide, but it had taught him the important fact that the prisoners were known less by their faces than by the numbers of their cells.

Escape seemed less and less remote, when a plan, bold and hazardous in its idea, crystallized from out the crude mass of projects with which his brain seethed. This was the plan – he would lag behind after service in chapel the next morning, conceal himself in a warder's pew, and lie in wait for the first official who might enter the chapel – such a one, in the graphic phrase of his disreputable friend, he would "knock out", and, seizing his keys and uniform, would explore the building. It would be too daring to attempt the passage of the gate, but it would be hard luck indeed if he discovered no ladder or other means of scaling the wall.

Such was his scheme in outline. He was keenly alive to its faultiness in detail; much, far too much, was left to chance – a slovenliness he had ever recoiled from. He felt that even the possession of the uniform would only give him the shortest time in which to work; and, while he risked the challenge of any casual warder who might detect his unfamiliar face, his ignorance of the way about would inevitably betray him before long. But his case could hardly be more desperate than at present; and, confident that if only he could hide himself in the chapel the first step to freedom would be gained, he lay down to rest in happier mood than had been his for two days past.

At the first stroke of the morning bell Pringle was on his feet, every nerve in tension, his brain thrilling with the one idea. In his morning freshness and vigour, and after a singularly dreamless sleep, all difficulties vanished as he recalled them, and even before the breakfast hour his impatient ear had already imagined the bell for chapel. When it did begin, and long before the warder was anywhere near his cell, Pringle was standing ready with his badge displayed and the little volumes in his hands.

The moment the door opened he was over the threshold; he had walked a yard or two on while the keys still rattled at the next cell; the man in front of him appeared to crawl, and the way seemed miles long. In his impatience he had taken a different place in the procession as compared with yesterday, and when at length he reached the haven and made for his old seat at the end of the bench against the wall he was promptly turned into the row in front of it. His first alarm that his plans were at the very outset frustrated gave way to delight as he found himself within a few inches only of the warder's pew without so much as a bench intervening, and, lest his thoughts might be palpable on his face, he feared to look up, but gazed intently on his open book.

The service dragged on and the chaplain's voice sounded drowsier than ever as he intoned the prayers, but the closing hymn was given out at last, and Pringle seized a welcome distraction by singing with a feverish energy which surprised himself. A pause, and then, while the organist resumed the air of the humn, the prisoners rose, bench after bench, and filed out.

The warder had passed from the pew towards the central aisle; he was watching his men out with face averted from Pringle. Now was the supreme moment. As his neighbours rose and turned their backs upon him, Pringle, with a rapid glance around, sidled down into the warder's pew and crouched along the bottom.

Deftly as he had slid into the confined space, the manoeuvre was not without incident − his collar burst upon the swelling muscles of his neck, and the stud with fiendish agility bounced to the floor, while quaking he listened to the rattle which should betray him. Seconds as long as minutes, minutes which seemed hours passed, and still the feet tramped endlessly along the floor. But now the organ ceased. Hesitating shuffles told the passing of some decrepit prisoner, last of the band, there was a jingling of keys, some coarse-worded remarks, a laugh, the snapping of a lock, and then − silence.

Pringle listened; he could hear nothing but the beating of his own heart. Slowly he raised himself above the edge of the desk and met the gaze of a burly man in a frogged tunic, who watched him with an amused expression upon his large round face.

"Lost anything?" inquired the big man with an air of interest.

"Yes, my liberty," Pringle was about to say bitterly, but, checking himself in time, he only replied, "My collar stud."

"Found it?"

For answer Pringle displayed it in his fingers, and then restored the accuracy of his collar and tie.

"Come this way," said the befrogged one, unlocking the door, and Pringle accepted the invitation meekly. Resistance would have been folly, and even had he been able to take his captor unawares, the possible outcome of a struggle with so heavy a man was by no means encouraging.

As the key turned upon Pringle and he found himself once more in the cell which he had left so hopefully but a short half-hour ago, he dropped despondently upon the stool, heedless of the exercise he was losing, incurious when in the course of the morning a youngish man in mufti entered the cell with the inquiry:

"Is your name Stammers?"

"Yes," Pringle wearily replied.

"You came in the night before last, I think? Did you complain of anything then?"

"Oh, no! Neither do I now." Pringle began to feel a little more interested in his visitor, whom he recognized as the doctor who had examined him on his arrival at the prison. "May I ask why you have come to see me?"

"I understand you are reported for a breach of discipline, and I have come to examine and certify you for punishment," was the somewhat officially dry answer.

"Indeed! I am unaware of having done anything particularly outrageous, but I suppose I shall be told?"

"Oh, yes; you'll be brought before the governor presently. Let me look at your tongue... Now just undo your waistcoat – and your shirt – a minute... Thanks, that will do."

The doctor's footsteps had died away along the gallery before Pringle quite realized that he had gone. So this was the result of his failure. He wondered what form the punishment would take. Well, he had tried and failed, and since nothing succeeds like success, so nothing would fail like failure, he supposed.

"Put on yer badge an' come along o' me."

It was the Irish warder speaking a few minutes later, and Pringle followed to his doom. At the end of the gallery they did not go up, as to chapel, nor down to the basement, as for exercise, but down one flight only to a clear space formed by the junction of the various blocks of the prison, which starred in half a dozen radiations to as many points of the compass.

As his eye travelled down the series of vistas with tier above tier of galleries running throughout and here and there a flying crossbridge, Pringle noted with dismay the uniformed figures at every turn, and the force of his fellow prisoner's remark as to the folly of a single-handed attempt to escape was brutally obvious.

He was roused by a touch on the shoulder. The Irish warder led him by the arm through the arched doorway along a dark passage, and thence into a large room with "Visiting Magistrates" painted on the door. Although certainly spacious, the greater part of the room was occupied by a species of cage, somewhat similar to that in which Pringle had been penned at the police court. Opening a gate therein the warder motioned him to enter and then drew himself up in stiff military pose at the side. Halfway down the table an elderly gentleman in morning dress, and wearing a closely cropped grey beard, sat reading a number of documents; beside him, the ponderous official who had shared Pringle's adventure in the chapel.

"Is this the man, chief warder?" inquired the gentleman. The chief warder testified to Pringle's identity, and "What is your name?" he continued.

"Give your name to the governor, now!" prompted the Irishman, as Pringle hesitated in renewed forgetfulness of his alias.

"Augustus Stammers, isn't it?" suggested the chief warder impatiently.

"Yes."

"You are remanded, I see," the governor observed, reading from a sheet of blue foolscap, "charged with unlawfully and knowingly uttering a piece of false and counterfeit coin resembling a florin." Pringle bowed, wondering what was coming next.

"You are reported to me, Stammers," continued the governor, "for having concealed yourself in the chapel after divine service, apparently with the intention of escaping. The chief warder states that he watched you from the gallery hide yourself in one of the officer's pews. What have you to say?"

"I can only say what I said to the chief warder. My collar stud burst while I was singing, and I lost it for ever so long. When I did find it in the warder's pew the chapel was empty."

"But were you looking for it when you hid yourself so carefully? And why did you wait for the warder to turn his back before you looked in the pew?"

"I only discovered it as we were about to leave the chapel. Even if I had tried to escape, I don't see the logic of reproving a man for obeying a natural instinct."

"I have no time to argue the point," the governor decided, "But I may tell you, if you are unaware of it, that it is an offence, punishable by statute, to escape from lawful custody. The magistrate has remanded you here, and here you must remain until he requires your presence at" – he picked up the foolscap sheet and glanced over it – "at the end of five more days. Your explanation is not altogether satisfactory, and I must caution you as to your future conduct. And let me advise you not to sing quite so loudly in chapel. Take him away."

"Outside!"

Stepping out of the cage Pringle was escorted back to the cell, congratulating himself on the light in which he had managed to present the affair. Still, he felt that his future movements were embarrassed; plausible as was the tale, the governor had made no attempt to conceal his suspicions, and Pringle inclined to think he was the object of a special surveillance when half a dozen times in the course of the afternoon he detected an eye at the spy-hole in the cell door. It was clear that he could do nothing further in his present position. He recalled the advice given him yesterday, and determined to "fetch the farm". There only could he break fresh ground; over there he might think of some new plan – perhaps concert it with another prisoner. Anyhow, he could not be worse off.

But here another difficulty arose. He was in good, even robust, health; and the doctor, having overhauled him twice recently, could hardly be imposed upon by any train of symptoms, be they never so harrowing in the recital.

Suddenly he recalled a statement from one of those true stories of prison life, always written by falsely-accused men – the number of innocent people who get sent to prison is really appalling!

It was on the extent to which soap-pills have been made to serve the purpose of the malingerer. Now the minute slab upon his shelf had always been repellent in external application, but for inward consumption – he hurriedly averted his gaze! But this was no time for fastidiousness; so, choosing the moment just after one of the periodical inspections of the warder, he hurriedly picked a corner from the stodgy cube, and, rolling it into a bolus, swallowed it with the help of repeated gulps of water. As a natural consequence, his appetite was not increased; and when supper arrived later on he contented himself with just sipping the tea, ignoring the brown loaf.

Sleep was long in coming to him that night; he knew that he was entering upon an almost hopeless enterprise, and his natural anxiety but enhanced the dyspeptic results of the strong alkali. Toward morning he dropped off; but when the bell rang at six there was little need for him to allege any symptoms of the malaise which was obvious in his pallor and his languid disinclination to rise.

"Ye'd better let me putt yer name down for the docthor, Stammers," was the not unkindly observation of the Irish warder as he collected. Pringle merely acquiesced with a nod, and when the chapel bell rang his cell door remained unopened.

"Worrying about anything?" suggested the doctor, as he entered the cell about an hour afterwards.

"Yes, I do feel rather depressed," the patient admitted.

A truthful narrative of the soap disease, amply corroborated by the medical examination, had the utmost effect which Pringle had dared to hope; and when, shortly after the doctor's visit, he was called out of the cell and bidden to leave his badge behind he was conscious of an exaltation of spirits giving an elasticity to his step which he was careful to conceal.

Along the passage, through a big oaken door, and then by a flight of steps they reached the paved courtyard. Right ahead of them the massive nail-studded gates were just visible through the inner ones which had clanged so dismally in Pringle's ears just three nights back.

"Fair truth, mate, 'ave I got the 'orrors? Tell us strite, d'yer see 'em?" In a whisper another and tremulous candidate for "the farm" pointed to the images of a pair of heraldic griffins which guarded the door; the sweat stood in great drops upon his face as he regarded the emblems of civic authority, and Pringle endeavoured to assure him of their reality until checked by a stern "Silence there!"

"Turn to the left," commanded the warder, who walked in the rear as with a flock of sheep.

From some distant part of the prison a jumbled score of men and women were trooping toward the gate. They were the friends of prisoners returning to the outside world after the brief daily visit allowed by the regulations, and as their paths converged towards the centre of the yard the free and the captive examined one another with equal interest.

"Ough!"… "Pore feller!"… "Old 'im up!"… "Git some water, do!"

The tremulous man had fallen to the ground with bloated, frothing features, his limbs wrenching and jerking convulsively. For a moment the two groups were intermingled, and then a little knot of four detached itself and staggered across the yard. A visitor, rushing from his place, had compassionately lifted the sufferer from the ground, and, with the warder and two assisting prisoners, disappeared through the hospital entrance.

In surly haste the visitors were again marshalled, and a warder beckoned Pringle to a place among them. For a brief second he hesitated. Surely the mistake would be at once discovered. Should he risk the forlorn chance? Was there time? He looked over to the hospital, but the Samaritan had not reappeared.

"Come on, will yer? Don't stand gaping there!" snarled the warder.

The head of the procession had already reached the inner gate; Pringle ran towards it, and was the last to enter the vestibule. Crash! He was on the right side of the iron gate when it closed this time.

"How many?" bawled the warder in the yard.

Deliberately the man counted them, and Pringle palpitated like a steamhammer. Would he never finish? What a swathe of red tape! At last! The wicket opened, another second – No, a woman squeezed in front of him; he must not seem too eager. Now! He gave a sob of relief.

In the approach a man holding a bundle of documents was discharging a cab. Pringle was inside it with a bound.

"Law Courts!" he gasped through the trap. "Half a sovereign if you do it quickly!"

A whistle blew shrilly as they passed the carriage gates. Swish – swish! went the whip. How the cab rocked! There was a shot behind. The policeman on point duty walked over from the opposite corner, but as the excited warders met him halfway across the road, the cab was already dwindling in the distance.

R Austin Freeman

The D'Arblay Mystery

When a man is found floating beneath the skin of a green-skimmed pond one morning, Dr Thorndyke becomes embroiled in an astonishing case. This wickedly entertaining detective fiction reveals that the victim was murdered through a lethal injection and someone out there is trying a cover-up.

Dr Thorndyke Intervenes

What would you do if you opened a package to find a man's head? What would you do if the headless corpse had been swapped for a case of bullion? What would you do if you knew a brutal murderer was out there, somewhere, and waiting for you? Some people would run. Dr Thorndyke intervenes.

R AUSTIN FREEMAN

FELO DE SE

John Gillam was a gambler. John Gillam faced financial ruin and was the victim of a sinister blackmail attempt. John Gillam is now dead. In this exceptional mystery, Dr Thorndyke is brought in to untangle the secrecy surrounding the death of John Gillam, a man not known for insanity and thoughts of suicide.

FLIGHTY PHYLLIS

Chronicling the adventures and misadventures of Phyllis Dudley, Richard Austin Freeman brings to life a charming character always getting into scrapes. From impersonating a man to discovering mysterious trap doors, *Flighty Phyllis* is an entertaining glimpse at the times and trials of a wayward woman.

R Austin Freeman

Helen Vardon's Confession

Through the open door of a library, Helen Vardon hears an argument that changes her life forever. Helen's father and a man called Otway argue over missing funds in a trust one night. Otway proposes a marriage between him and Helen in exchange for his co-operation and silence. What transpires is a captivating tale of blackmail, fraud and death. Dr Thorndyke is left to piece together the clues in this enticing mystery.

Mr Pottermack's Oversight

Mr Pottermack is a law-abiding, settled homebody who has nothing to hide until the appearance of the shadowy Lewison, a gambler and blackmailer with an incredible story. It appears that Pottermack is in fact a runaway prisoner, convicted of fraud, and Lewison is about to spill the beans unless he receives a large bribe in return for his silence. But Pottermack protests his innocence, and resolves to shut Lewison up once and for all. Will he do it? And if he does, will he get away with it?

OTHER TITLES BY R AUSTIN FREEMAN AVAILABLE DIRECT
FROM HOUSE OF STRATUS

Quantity	£	$(US)	$(CAN)	€
A Certain Dr Thorndyke	6.99	12.95	19.95	13.50
The D'Arblay Mystery	6.99	12.95	19.95	13.50
Dr Thorndyke Intervenes	6.99	12.95	19.95	13.50
Dr Thorndyke's Casebook	6.99	12.95	19.95	13.50
The Eye of Osiris	6.99	12.95	19.95	13.50
Felo De Se	6.99	12.95	19.95	13.50
Flighty Phyllis	6.99	12.95	19.95	13.50
The Golden Pool: A Story of a Forgotten Mine	6.99	12.95	19.95	13.50
The Great Portrait Mystery	6.99	12.95	19.95	13.50
Helen Vardon's Confession	6.99	12.95	19.95	13.50

ALL HOUSE OF STRATUS BOOKS ARE AVAILABLE FROM GOOD BOOKSHOPS
OR DIRECT FROM THE PUBLISHER:

Internet: www.houseofstratus.com including synopses and features.

Email: sales@houseofstratus.com please quote author, title and credit card details.

OTHER TITLES BY R AUSTIN FREEMAN AVAILABLE DIRECT
FROM HOUSE OF STRATUS

Quantity	£	$(US)	$(CAN)	€
MR POLTON EXPLAINS	6.99	12.95	19.95	13.50
MR POTTERMACK'S OVERSIGHT	6.99	12.95	19.95	13.50
THE MYSTERY OF 31 NEW INN	6.99	12.95	19.95	13.50
THE MYSTERY OF ANGELINA FROOD	6.99	12.95	19.95	13.50
THE PENROSE MYSTERY	6.99	12.95	19.95	13.50
THE PUZZLE LOCK	6.99	12.95	19.95	13.50
THE RED THUMB MARK	6.99	12.95	19.95	13.50
THE SHADOW OF THE WOLF	6.99	12.95	19.95	13.50
A SILENT WITNESS	6.99	12.95	19.95	13.50
THE SINGING BONE	6.99	12.95	19.95	13.50
WHEN ROGUES FALL OUT	6.99	12.95	19.95	13.50

ALL HOUSE OF STRATUS BOOKS ARE AVAILABLE FROM GOOD BOOKSHOPS
OR DIRECT FROM THE PUBLISHER:

Order Line: UK: 0800 169 1780,
USA: 1 800 509 9942
INTERNATIONAL: +44 (0) 20 7494 6400 (UK)
or +01 212 218 7649
(please quote author, title, and credit card details.)

Send to: House of Stratus Sales Department   House of Stratus Inc.
24c Old Burlington Street   Suite 210
London   1270 Avenue of the Americas
W1X 1RL   New York • NY 10020
UK   USA

PAYMENT

Please tick currency you wish to use:

☐ £ (Sterling)   ☐ $ (US)   ☐ $ (CAN)   ☐ € (Euros)

Allow for shipping costs charged per order plus an amount per book as set out in the tables below:

CURRENCY/DESTINATION

	£(Sterling)	$(US)	$(CAN)	€(Euros)
Cost per order				
UK	1.50	2.25	3.50	2.50
Europe	3.00	4.50	6.75	5.00
North America	3.00	3.50	5.25	5.00
Rest of World	3.00	4.50	6.75	5.00
Additional cost per book				
UK	0.50	0.75	1.15	0.85
Europe	1.00	1.50	2.25	1.70
North America	1.00	1.00	1.50	1.70
Rest of World	1.50	2.25	3.50	3.00

PLEASE SEND CHEQUE OR INTERNATIONAL MONEY ORDER.
payable to: STRATUS HOLDINGS plc or HOUSE OF STRATUS INC. or card payment as indicated

STERLING EXAMPLE

Cost of book(s):..................... Example: 3 x books at £6.99 each: £20.97

Cost of order: .... Example: £1.50 (Delivery to UK address)

Additional cost per book:............. Example: 3 x £0.50: £1.50

Order total including shipping:........... Example: £23.97

VISA, MASTERCARD, SWITCH, AMEX:

☐☐☐☐☐☐☐☐☐☐☐☐☐☐☐☐☐☐

Issue number (Switch only):

☐☐☐

Start Date: **Expiry Date:**

☐☐/☐☐   ☐☐/☐☐

Signature: _____

NAME: _____

ADDRESS: _____

COUNTRY: _____

ZIP/POSTCODE: _____

Please allow 28 days for delivery. Despatch normally within 48 hours.

Prices subject to change without notice.
Please tick box if you do not wish to receive any additional information. ☐

House of Stratus publishes many other titles in this genre; please check our website (**www.houseofstratus.com**) for more details.